HER SECRET lover

A WHAT HAPPENS IN VEGAS STORY

ROBIN COVINGTON

Entangled Publishing, LLC
2614 South Timberline Road
Suite 109
Fort Collins, CO 80525
Visit our website at www.entangledpublishing.com.

Lovestruck is an imprint of Entangled Publishing, LLC.

Edited by Alethea Spiridon Hopson
Cover design by Heather Howland
Cover art from iStock

Manufactured in the United States of America

First Edition January 2016

Chapter One

Who knew a box of dildos would weigh so much?

Kelsey Kyle watched her reflection juggle her parcels in the high-gloss metal of the elevator doors as she headed to the VIP level of the Masquerade Hotel and Casino in Las Vegas. Yeah, she could have taken the cart offered to her by "Pervy" Dave who worked as a bellhop, but he got her hackles up, and she didn't want to accept any of his assistance. Now, she was regretting her decision.

Of course the elevator stopped at almost every floor and dumped out passengers as she made her way to the Executive Level concierge floor, where they were housing the VIP guests of the eighteenth annual Romance Lovers' Convention. The actual event didn't start for two days, but already attendees were pouring into Sin City to either enjoy the nightlife or to set up displays and have meetings.

It was because of the early arrival of the folks from Love You Big Time that she was rising above the ground forty floors carrying enough sex toys to keep an orgy going for at least a couple of days. Once again, she'd saved the day for a guest and even Perry, the second shift Head Concierge, had to offer up one of his smiles that never quite showed in his eyes.

"Fuck you too, Perry," she muttered under her breath, remembering at the last moment that she wasn't alone in the elevator.

She glanced over and smiled at the older couple wearing sandals with socks and carrying bags with labels from some of the pricier tourist traps, and wished they'd come to the concierge to ask about where to shop. As a lifelong Las Vegan, she knew where to go to get the best and cheapest *anything*. It was why she was always the most highly rated Junior Concierge at the Masquerade and why she was a shoo-in for the spot in the management trainee program. She'd worked her ass off for years, during college and after, to get to this point.

The spot in the program and the subsequent job at the Masquerade would give her extra cash to pay for her mother's special medical care. With her dad still working, her share was more than enough, but he wanted to retire and she wanted him to take it easy for a change. She took a moment to send a prayer to Lady Luck, the patron saint of Las Vegas.

"Have a great day," she said to the couple as they got off on their floor and waved. The doors slid shut and she adjusted the heavy box again as her Bluetooth device beeped in her ear. Kelsey threw up a silent prayer of thanks that the device was voice-activated, because there was no way in hell she could let go of the box to tap a button. "This is Kyle."

Perry's voice, even insincere over the wireless, assaulted her ear. "Kyle, you need to come back down here when you're done delivering the parcels. We have a special request from a high-roller VIP, and since you're so used to playing Supergirl, it's yours."

She stuck her tongue out at him even though he couldn't see it. He never failed to give her a hard time. She would have been ass hurt about it, but he treated everyone the same way. It was like he was always waiting for someone to make that *one mistake* so he could throw it up in their face for eternity. But she didn't make mistakes, and she would always do whatever it took to get the job done. If the request was impossible, she got the guest the next best thing or something better. She was that good.

"I'll grab my cape and fly on down as soon as I've completed my deliveries," she said.

"Uh huh," he grunted into the phone and disconnected.

She refrained from verbalizing the thoughts running through her head, since she wasn't one hundred percent sure that he couldn't tap into the security feed in the elevator, but she thought them…oh yes, she did. The cab stopped at her floor, and she heaved out a sigh of exertion as she readjusted the box and prepared to step out onto the Executive Level. Once she was in possible sight of guests, she needed to be professional and poised. A perfect example of the superb hospitality offered by the Masquerade.

A quick *ding* and *swoosh* of the metal doors and Kelsey put one high-heeled pump on the plush carpet and walked as briskly down the hall as she could, stopping in front of the suite currently occupied by Micah Holmes, the *New York Times* bestselling novelist and hermit. He'd checked in the previous Friday night, and the only evidence that he was still alive was the requests for extra towels, and orders placed to room service and Barakoa, the coffee shop. According to her review of his file, Mr. Holmes loved his bath linen plentiful and his caffeine "black, strong, and not filled with any of that hipster sweet crap."

Good to know. And it was her job to know since he would be her responsibility from today until the conclusion of the romance convention. The fact that he was her very favorite author had nothing to do with the flutter in the pit of her stomach.

"Professional, Kelsey. Not a fangirl," she muttered to herself.

Kelsey pressed the buzzer next to the door and waited, listening to the sound of footsteps on the marble floor in the foyer of the suite. The lock tumbled and it swung open to reveal a tall man wearing a black T-shirt that read "I'm still kind of mad they never actually told us how to get to Sesame Street." The snort of laughter pushed past her lips before she could stop it but immediately dried up in her throat when her eyes traveled back up and got a long, full look at his face.

Micah Holmes was fucking hot.

Gorgeous. Dark eyes framed by heavy-rimmed glasses, cleft chin peeking out from the several days' growth of beard, and dark, coffee-colored hair sticking up in a way that should have been funny but only succeeded in looking sexy and rumpled. She let her gaze travel back down his torso, and she realized the shirt was pulled taut against his muscled chest and strained against the flex of his bicep.

Kelsey was a romance novel junkie and had read his books many times over and stared at his photo on the back just as often, but he looked…different. Better. Hotter. Maybe if he actually resembled the awful, stuffy author headshot on the back of his books, then she wouldn't be staring at him like she'd missed breakfast, lunch, and dinner right now.

And he was staring back at her. His eyes made one long journey from her hair to her shoes and then made the return trip, stopping to look her right in the eyes.

"Wow," he said, and she actually saw the blush creep across his cheeks.

"Hi," she said, biting back the eye roll when she realized she sounded like an idiot, but it didn't stop her from continuing to stare.

"Is that for me?" Micah asked, his voice low and even, with more than a hint of a southern twang. It was a deep and rich with an edge of gravel from either too much caffeine or too little sleep. When he made to reach for the box, she snapped out of her stupor and remembered to do her job.

"I'm sorry, Mr. Holmes. I'm Kelsey Kyle, a junior concierge here at the Masquerade. May I come in?"

When he nodded and stood to the side, she entered the room, immediately looking for a spot to place the box as she conducted her business. The suite was formed in the shape of an arc, with an open living space on one side and the bed hidden behind an ornate wall. Every spot featured a stunning view of the strip, and the room also had a rooftop deck with a hot tub and sitting area.

"May I place these here for a moment, Mr. Holmes?" she asked, indicating an open spot on the long table situated behind the couch. It was the only space without something already placed on it. A laptop computer took up the coffee table, along with piles of paper and a printer. Other papers and books and newspapers were strewn over every surface in the space. It was…a mess.

Micah Holmes was a slob, and she even thought that was hot. Jesus.

"Here, let me help you." He walked over, and she realized refusing would be wasted on a guy bred with southern gentleman manners, so she let him take the boxes and put them on the tabletop. She watched him, only ogling a little when his shirt hitched up on the side, and she got a glimpse of the top of that arrow thing above a man's hips that seemed like God's unnecessary-but-appreciated-GPS-direction to where the best bits were. He straightened up and turned quickly, and their eyes caught as she moved her gaze back to areas more appropriate for a guest of the hotel.

"Thank you, Mr. Holmes." Kelsey reached over and picked up the package meant for him, a large padded envelope that felt like a ream of paper was inside. "I need you to sign for this."

She held it out to him while she searched in her inside jacket pocket for the pen she always kept there before remembering she'd stuffed it into her other pocket earlier on during her shift. She retrieved it and looked up to hand it over when she caught him staring at her…well, a part of her. Her breasts in particular, where they peeked out above the edge of her camisole.

Her hand remained suspended in midair as she watched his cheeks flush red when he realized he'd been caught. She lifted her lips in a tentative smile, trying to keep it on the correct side of professional but finding it hard since all of her female bits were outrageously pleased with the attention. Fraternizing with a guest was the fastest way to get your ass fired.

"Mr. Holmes," she said, raising the pen higher in to his line of sight. He shook his head slightly and took the pen from her hand, his fingers brushing against her own and tempting her to linger. If it had been off-hours, she would have held on to it, flirting as she dragged out the contact, but not right now.

"I'm sorry." He took the paper and signed it, indicating he'd received the package and handed it back to her. When he looked at her and offered her the paper, his smile was crooked, and she noticed that one of his bottom front teeth was chipped. So he wasn't perfect… "I've lost my manners being cooped up in here for five days."

"You should get out and see the Strip. I can recommend lots of places to you. I grew up in Las Vegas."

"Oh, I'm not really a Strip kind of guy." He shoved his hands into the pockets of his jeans, breaking eye contact and glancing out at the view. "I was thinking of taking a guided hike in the desert, but time got away from me."

"Well, I'm your assigned, personal concierge starting today and for the duration of the convention, so if you can squeeze in the time, I'll be happy to arrange it."

His head whipped up and he smiled, and she couldn't help but smile back as she handed him her card. His grin was…warm, heating her up down to her bones. "My personal concierge?"

"Yes. I'll help you with whatever you need during the convention. Reservations, excursions, assistance at conference events. You call me, and I'll help you. Okay, Mr. Holmes?"

He examined her card and then shoved it in a pocket. His smile was still warm, his gaze roaming a little. She fought the urge to make sure her hair still looked good and her skirt was straight. It didn't matter what she looked like; he wasn't a prospective boyfriend. He was a guest.

"Call me Micah," he said.

"I can't," she said, rushing to explain when he frowned. "We aren't allowed to call guests by their first names."

"Oh, okay," he said, his brow scrunched up like he was going to argue. "I don't want to get you in trouble."

"I appreciate that, Mr. Holmes." She had to admit to herself that it sounded dumb using his full name when he was only five or six years older, but those were the rules for the job she needed to get back to sooner rather than later. She resisted the urge to check her watch and patted the top of her remaining delivery. "Well, I need to get these to the guests down the hall. I'm here until eight tonight, and after that the on-duty concierge will help you or you can leave a message for me to retrieve tomorrow. Sound good?"

Kelsey turned and lifted the box from the table, and she felt and heard it as the bottom ripped open. Like one of those scenes in a movie, everything slowed down to a crawl as the dildos, butt plugs, and things she didn't know what they did—or where they went—fell all over the floor. Some of them switched on, buzzing like bumblebees as they rolled and bounced and spread out like sexual floodwaters across the marble floor.

"Oh my God," she yelled, dropping the box and hitting her knees on the floor as she desperately tried to scoop them all back into the container at once.

"What the hell?" Micah landed on the floor beside her, joining in the mission to capture the escaping sex toys. His long arms had better reach than she did but there were so many. Red, yellow, pink, black, and even purple glitter in every shape, length, and size imaginable.

They both reached out and grabbed the same dildo at the same time. At least nine inches long and so big around that her fingers didn't meet, it was black with embedded gold glitter and it vibrated so hard her teeth rattled. She looked up at him and opened her mouth to apologize but had no idea what to say.

"Holy hell, Kelsey, it's like a horny Crayola box exploded all over the floor," he said with a flush in his cheeks that matched her own. He tugged on the sex toy and she released it, watching in horror as he read the tag. "Big Daddy Dildo. Use lots of lube." He grinned at her. "That's good advice, especially depending on where you plan to put it."

It was too much.

He snickered. She giggled. They both burst out in laughter, big belly laughs that brought tears to her eyes that she tried to blink back to spare her eye makeup. Micah fell back on his ass, the dildo still buzzing away in his hand as he snorted with gut-busting laughter.

It was not professional. Not the cool exterior she worked so hard to maintain on the job.

"Oh damn," he said, reaching up to wipe away his own tears and almost poked himself in the eye with the silicone cockhead. That made her laugh harder, and it continued for several long minutes until they could finally get themselves together.

"Please tell me that these aren't all yours," he said with a last snort.

She shook her head, finally catching her breath. "No. Oh God, no. The vendors from the sex toy company Love You Big Time practically collapsed in panic at my feet in the concierge office when they realized their demo items had been lost somewhere in Utah, and their usual sources were either out of stock or couldn't get them here in time. My best friend, Sarina, owns a local adult toy store, and she sent over what they needed."

"Your best friend owns a sex shop?" He picked up a cherry red butt plug and squeezed the bulb attached by a long piece of tubing, his eyes going wide and his cheeks even redder when the plug expanded. The more he squeezed the bigger it got, and she found herself wondering at what point it moved from *that feels good* to *get it out now*. "Damn. All I can think of is how much that would hurt if you overinflated it and it popped while you were…um…using it."

"Well, I guess you better read the directions first to make sure that doesn't happen."

"My Y chromosome makes it impossible for me to read directions. It all looks like Farsi or Martian." He jumped a little when he pressed a button and the toy deflated with a loud burp. "Jesus."

"You're excused," she said on a laugh, realizing too late she'd just made a fart joke with a guest holding an inflatable butt plug. She hoped to God this didn't make it onto the guest feedback card at the end of his trip.

"I shouldn't have had the burrito for lunch," he said, continuing his retrieval of the sex toys on the floor. She continued to snort unprofessionally when she really should get a grip on herself.

Kelsey held up the box, frowning at the bottom where it was split open along the flaps. He glanced up and peered through the opening at her.

"Hold on, I think I have a box you can use." Micah scrambled to his feet and disappeared behind the bar that separated the kitchenette area from the rest of the suite. She continued to locate the ones buzzing on the floor and turned them off as he bumped around in search of a box. "Found it! My publisher sent a few books for me to sign."

She looked up as he rounded the corner with a box about the same size as the one that had failed her so miserably. He held it out but tugged the container back when she reached out.

"Wait." He lifted his lip in the sexy half-smile that she already liked seeing on his face. Its heat contrasted in the best way with the shy, dark brown cast of his eyes and the reserved but warm lilt of his accent. She knew where his heroes got their ability to make every heroine fall for them so hard. He looked in the mirror. "If I give you this box, I want something in return."

Kelsey tried to frown but it was impossible. He was having too much fun and he had her interest piqued, but she was also suspicious. Usually when a guest said that to her, there were serious strings attached and often of the sexual variety.

"What do you want?"

"I want you to call me Micah." When she opened her mouth to protest he cut her off. "Not in public. I don't want you to get in trouble, but if it's just the two of us, don't call me Mr. Holmes. I feel like I need to pull out a pipe and find a sidekick named Watson every time someone calls me that."

She'd thought he was going to ask her out, and she recognized the bite of disappointment in her gut. There was no denying their attraction to each other, and she'd grown accustomed to men in Vegas for a few days not wasting any time to go after what they wanted; she'd arrogantly expected that he was the same. It wasn't like she could accept him anyway.

First, there was the "no fraternization with the guests" rule at the Masquerade. If she was caught, she would be fired and that was something she couldn't even fathom. She loved her job. Second was her own rule to never get involved with a Vegas tourist ever again. She'd been burned too many times by men who took off their wedding rings or forgot their commitments back home the minute they hit the airport terminal. Kelsey had learned the hard way that "what happens in Vegas, stays in Vegas" meant the girl you romanced morning, noon, and night. The only thing that stayed behind in Vegas was her broken heart.

He was waiting for her answer, and she decided she could give him this. At the Masquerade the guest was always right, and this request was harmless.

"You drive a hard bargain, Mr. Holmes." She couldn't help teasing him and let a laugh loose when he narrowed his eyes and refused to let the box go. "Fine, *Micah.*"

"I don't know why that had to be so hard." He squatted down and helped her place the sex toys in the box, using a long pink one to emphasize his point. "After you've shared a sex toy, you *have* to be on a first-name basis."

"When we aren't within earshot of other guests or my boss."

"Of course." He plopped the last dildo in the box and stood, holding out his hand to help her to her feet. She took it gratefully, knowing that if she tried to get up on her own she'd run the risk of letting Micah know exactly what she wore underneath the black pencil skirt of her uniform. He leaned over, picked it up, and handed her the box. "Do you need a hand delivering this orgy-in-a-box?"

"No. Thank you, but no." Kelsey took the box from him and found herself staring up in to his face, answering his grin with one of her own. She knew she should back up and put her professional mask on, although it was hard to do when she stood holding a box of butt plugs next to a really cute guy who made her laugh. "I'll be off to make my…delivery. I'll be in touch about the convention, but remember to give me a call if you need anything."

Micah gave her another flash of his grin as he shoved his hands in his pockets. "I'll be seeing you, Kelsey Kyle."

And she was looking forward to it.

Chapter Two

"Micah, when are you going to be done with this damn book?"

He sat on the sofa and watched Allen George, his agent, pace back and forth over the marble floor of his suite. Micah knew better than to interrupt him when he was trying to bully him into delivering the manuscript early. He reached over and grabbed his beer off the coffee table, taking a sip before settling back against the cushions.

"Allen, I've been here since Friday doing nothing but work on the damn book. Nobody wants to be done more than I do." And God knew that was the truth. If he could go back five years and never answer the ad for a ghostwriter, he would. Micah would have taken the fucking note handed to him by his creative writing teacher and used it for target practice.

"Will this one really be the last? Are you still going turn down eight figures and make me a poor man? Do you have any idea how much fifteen percent of a gazillion dollars actually is? Do you?"

"I think math is *your* job," he said.

"Fifteen percent of a gazillion dollars is enough for me to build two pools at my house in Turks and Caicos."

"Fuck you, Allen." Micah laughed, throwing a pillow at the man who'd become his friend over the years. He was greedy, loud, and obnoxiously extravagant with women, sports tickets, and cars. The total opposite of Micah, but he'd not had a better friend since his time in the Marines. "I've made you very rich over the years. How much money do you need?"

"More," Allen said as he threw himself down on the couch. "And it's not about *needing* the money, Mike. You know that." He tipped his own beer back and shook his head. "I don't know how you can turn down that kind of money for three more books."

"It's easy because I don't want to write these fucking books anymore. I never meant for this to be my career, and it won't matter how much money they throw at it."

"All right, all right." Allen held up his hands in surrender. They'd had this conversation a million times, drunk, sober, hungover, in person and on the phone.

"Sell my military thriller and make sure you can continue to live up to the level to which you've become accustomed, princess."

"That hurts, asshole." Allen grabbed at his chest. "It's true, but it hurts."

"I'll call down to front desk and get you a *Hello Kitty* Band-Aid."

Allen sighed, his frustration evident, sending a kick of unease to Micah's gut. This wasn't just a social call, and his friend didn't have good news. He reached over, picked up his beer, and took a long swallow. He was pretty sure he would need all the alcohol he could get for this conversation.

"Micah, we have no offers on your book unless you agree

to write romance for the house as well," Allen said, his tone more of an apology than anything else. Of course he would think that this was his fault.

"Well, that fucking sucks, but it's not your fault."

"It's my job to sell your books. I think the blame lies completely in my lap." He shoved Micah in the shoulder. "It doesn't mean I won't keep trying if that's what you really want."

"That's what I really want." He sighed and leaned his head against the back cushions of the sofa, staring at the overly carved ceiling of this outrageously overpriced suite. "I know it's shitty to turn down that kind of money, but I don't want to be obligated to write anymore of these books. I really don't want to do it."

Allen was quiet on his end of the couch, the only sound the *thunk* of his beer bottle being placed on the table.

"This is what I don't get, man. How do you write these incredible books when you don't believe in love? They are the most romantic shit ever put between two covers. You write the 'books that make America fall in love' for Christ's sake."

"I hate that stupid tagline…"

"You can hate it all you want, but it's true. You even get me weepy when I read them." His friend smacked him on the shoulder. "We've been friends long enough that I can tell you I thought you had a vagina after I read your first book."

That got his attention. He swiveled his head to glare at his best friend. "What the hell are you talking about?"

"I'm just saying I didn't believe a guy wrote them when I first read them." He held his pointer finger up to forestall the comment Micah wanted to make. "I know you don't actually *have* a vagina. I've seen you at the gym and you've got plenty going on down there to make the rest of us feel bad."

"Stop looking at my dick, Allen. Seriously."

"I only looked that one time, and you're missing my

point."

"You have one?" He snorted and ducked another jab that almost made him spill his beer. "I've been writing for a solid week, please don't make me read your mind."

Allen got up and headed over to the kitchen area, opening the refrigerator to get another beer. He removed the bottle cap before he continued. "My point is that you write this shit that gets every woman in America crying and then climbing on top of their husbands who immediately start begging their doctors for Viagra by the truckload, and I don't know how you do it when you don't date…"

"My lifestyle doesn't make it feasible."

"You don't have a sex life to speak of…"

"As long as my hands aren't amputated, my sex life is fine."

"That's pathetic and disturbing," Allen said and took a swig from his beer bottle. "But what I don't get is how you don't believe in love and you still write books that sell like ammo during the zombie apocalypse."

Micah thought about explaining all the shit in his head about love and life and what went through his mind when he sat down to write a book, but he'd have to get into Becky and his marriage and his divorce and the Marines and getting blown up, and he didn't want to go there. Not today. It wasn't that he didn't believe in love, it just wasn't easy to find, and to make it last was even rarer.

After he'd become successful, women had been plentiful and aggressive, perfect for a guy who was shy and still bearing the scorch marks from his divorce. He'd had to make very little effort to gain a woman in his life. A few attempts to jump back into sex and relationships and he'd learned the hard way that women either wanted his money or expected him to be the hero in their favorite book. One look at his modest lifestyle, and conversation that didn't sound like a script, and they were gone, pissed off like they'd been sold a bill of goods.

After those terrible experiences, he'd given up dating. Nothing killed the mood faster than wondering what the person you were with *really* wanted from you.

"It's not hard to sell the happily ever after in four hundred pages," he said and finished off his beer.

It was trying to make it work beyond that first kiss, the wedding photos, and the life of real-time epilogue that was hard. Bills, deployments, children, in-laws, and the day-to-day stuff were what happened next. Couples who made it that far were rare.

Allen stared at him from across the room, waiting to see if he was going to say more, but he just shrugged. That was all he had.

"Okay, back to the books. Have you taken another look at the business proposal I put together for setting up your own publishing company and self-publishing your books?" Allen asked and Micah groaned.

"I don't want to have to run a company. Hire people. I just don't."

"But you might have to. I wouldn't be much of an agent if I didn't tell you the cold hard truth."

"You want to stay and have dinner?" Micah asked. He'd eaten every meal for five days by himself, and he could use a little company. He normally preferred his own company, but even he had to surface from the cave every now and then and make a human connection.

"I can't. There are a couple of publishers here already, and I set up drinks and dinner with them. Sorry."

"No worries. I should stay in and work on the book anyway." He briefly thought of Kelsey, wondering if it would be too stalkerish to call her up and ask her to have dinner with him.

"The convention organizers will touch base with you

tomorrow and will coordinate all the events with the personal concierge the hotel is providing for you," Allen said as he swiped over the screen on his phone. "I'm trying to find her name and contact info to send you."

"Kelsey. Her name is Kelsey Kyle," he said, enjoying the look of shock on Allen's face. "I have her card. She dropped it off earlier."

Allen glanced around the room, surveying the mess with a shake of his head. "You had a woman in here? And you spoke to her?"

Micah sighed, dropping his empty bottle in the trash and leaned on the granite countertop of the bar. He wasn't going to argue with Allen and his observation. He wasn't good with women. He never really knew what to say and when they expected him to be one of the heroes of his books—or worse, the actors who played them in the movie version—it was never a good scene.

"She was really easy to talk to." He laughed remembering how they'd met. "After she dropped her box of dildos and butt plugs on the floor, it wasn't that hard to talk to her even though she is one of the prettiest women I've ever seen."

And for a man who made his living with words, "pretty" was the best he could do with the way she made him a little tongue-tied. Kelsey's skin was a flawless caramel complemented by copper-colored eyes and full, plump lips that easily curved into a smile. Her cheeks and the upper part of her chest flushed pink with embarrassment, but a dimple appeared on the right side of her mouth when she laughed. Long, dark hair fell to the middle of her back and had a slight wave. With her heels on, the top of her head reached his shoulder, which meant she was much shorter than his six feet four inches in height. He could go on and on. The problem had been noticing all the things about her that made her beautiful but trying not to get caught.

"Wait." Allen held up his hand and gave him a disbelieving look. He started counting off on his fingers to emphasize his point. "You had a pretty woman in here who was easy for you to talk to, *and* she brought her own butt plug?"

He smiled. "Yep."

"You need to marry her and find out if she has a sister for me."

"I *was* thinking about asking her to have dinner with me," he said, knowing he was going to get the exact reaction he received.

"Who are you? Really?"

"Fuck off, and don't give me shit about it. You're always telling me to get back out there and now I'm thinking about it, I don't need your crap."

"What are you going to do? Charm this girl and whisk her off to the backwoods of Bridger Gap?"

"What? No." Micah shook his head at that ridiculous comment. He wasn't sure he was ever going to be ready to take a walk down the twisted path to love ever again. When you got burned like he did, to describe him as skittish was an understatement. "Allen, I'm not talking about hearts, flowers, and a quickie wedding down on the Strip, but as you pointed out, I need to get laid."

He thought about how long it had been for him. Almost a year. The last time had been with the woman who'd posted a picture of him sleeping the next morning with a caption that said he fucked like his heroes…long and hard. Nice. That had been really fun to explain to his mom.

"If you need to get off, I can get you a—"

Micah cut him off before he could even finish that sentence. "I don't pay for sex. Jesus."

Allen watched him closely, his eyes assessing and making Micah feel like a bug under some kid's magnifying glass in the heat of summer. He could feel the impact of his friend's scrutiny, and he knew Allen was making plans and wondering what he could do to help Micah along.

Just. No.

"Allen, I'm serious. Back off. You're my agent, not a pimp, and you have horrible taste in women."

His friend was not pleased with the "down boy," but he acknowledged the order with a shrug as he pocketed his cell phone. "Fine, but you better tell me if this thing with the girl becomes something I *can* make a big deal about."

Micah smiled and promised himself that he would follow through and ask her out. There weren't many women who tempted him, but Kelsey Kyle was on the top of the short list. "Allen, you'll be the third person to know."

Chapter Three

"Ms. Kelsey Kyle, let me introduce you to Saul and Babette Forasch," Perry said.

Kelsey put on her best smile as she extended her hand to the couple seated on the plush sofa in the luxuriously appointed VIP concierge suite. She'd met Saul before: he was a frequent high roller here at the Masquerade and was very demanding. The last time he'd been a guest she'd had to arrange the delivery of four Gray's Papaya hot dogs from New York City with less than six hours notice because he wanted them for a late-night, after-the-poker-game snack. While the adventure had curled her hair with stress, she'd really appreciated the five hundred dollar tip he'd given her.

"Mr. Forasch, it is so nice to see you again," she said as she turned to greet the sixth Mrs. Forasch. Babette was probably Kelsey's age with huge breasts and red hair that defied gravity, and was covered from head to toe in designer clothes and bling. She screamed "trophy wife," and it was a testament to Saul's prenuptial agreements that he could afford to keep her in the style most gold diggers wanted to attain. "Congratulations on your marriage, Mrs. Forasch. I've arranged for a sensual couples massage in the penthouse as a gift from the Masquerade. You tell me the time, and I'll make it happen."

"Saul"—Babette nudged her husband and purred with a generous portion of a whine—"tell her what I *really* want."

Kelsey was glad for so many years of practice in hiding her candid reactions from guests, because it took a lot of effort to ensure that the Forasches didn't see her teeth clenching at the sound of her voice. Nails on a chalkboard and failing brakes were more soothing than Babette's childish tone.

"Of course, I will strive to get you anything your heart desires while you are guests at the Masquerade," she said, leaving the "as long as you don't mind the bill" unsaid. Dreams were never free, especially in Las Vegas.

"My wife wanted to come here to attend the Romance Lovers' Convention. She loves those books, and I love reaping the benefits of all those sex scenes." Saul leered at his wife and pulled her close. "If you know what I mean."

Ew. Yeah, they all knew what he meant. Kelsey sneaked a glance at Perry, who was clearly trying not to throw up. "I think we all know what you mean."

"Well, Babette is a huge fan of this guy, Micah Holmes, and she wants one of those 'Ultimate Fan' packages with him." He leaned over and licked his wife's ear, and Kelsey could not stop the shiver of revulsion. "She wants to spend the day with him, go to dinner, hang out."

"I want an early copy of his next book." Babette pouted and actually batted her fake eyelashes. They resembled two dead butterflies stuck to her eyeballs.

"Don't we all," Kelsey muttered before she smiled and broke the bad news. The hotel had repeatedly asked Micah to participate in the packages they put together to showcase the convention, but his agent had been firm that he was not interested. "Mr. Holmes declined our numerous requests for that package, but I would be happy to try to arrange it with any of the other authors attending the convention."

"I thought you were Supergirl." Saul turned and repeated his pseudo question to Perry. "You said she was Supergirl."

Perry opened his mouth to respond, but she didn't want him to open his big yap.

"Supergirl, yes. A magician, no." She smiled at Saul and Babette, using her most persuasive tone. It worked on an Arab sheikh once, and she bet it could work on a guy from L.A. who owned a suspect import/export business. "Mr. Holmes's representative made it very clear that he is not available for the Ultimate Fan experience."

"Maybe you could ask him again since you're his personal concierge," Perry said, every syllable dripping with "I got ya." She turned and glared at him, but he was undeterred. "He might change his mind."

Saul was not a man to pass up an opening like that. "I'll sweeten the pot for you and guarantee you an excellent reference for the management trainee program you told me about the last time I was here."

"What? You remember that?" she asked, stunned that he recalled a conversation that happened over four months ago.

"I always remember things that I might be able to use as leverage later." He twisted his lips in a smile that creeped her out. It was the kind of line guys in films delivered right before they slapped duct tape over a girl's mouth and shoved her in the trunk of a car. "You make this happen for my Babette, and I'll give you a reference that would get Satan back into heaven."

"Jesus," she said, letting her polish slip with her shock.

"He's already there," Saul joked as he rose to his feet with Babette.

"Tell Micah I'm his biggest fan," Babette said and reached

out to squeeze Kelsey's hand with another flutter of the dead butterflies.

Kelsey was torn. Micah had been adamant about not participating, and she dreaded bringing it up again, but they'd shared a connection earlier, and maybe she could persuade him to change his mind. It should probably make her stomach turn to think about using their obvious attraction to get what she needed, but it wouldn't be the first time she used whatever advantage she had to seal the deal. It's how things worked in Vegas. It couldn't be the first time Micah was asked to do it—it was part of his job with his publisher. With a little time, she guessed she could persuade him. She nodded.

"I'll do my best, Mr. and Mrs. Forasch."

She watched them leave, Babette chattering on about going to shop at Chanel and Harry Winston.

"I feel like I should call and warn Carla at Chanel," Perry said, his voice carrying a derisive tone he would have never used in front of a guest. They had personal contacts all over the city, and the very nice woman at Chanel would definitely appreciate a heads-up that Saul and Babette were on their way.

"For a man who works in hospitality, you really don't seem to like people all that much," Kelsey said, turning to face the guy who'd just thrown her under the bus.

"I *don't* like most people. Just a select few."

"Well, I'm clearly not one of the select few for you to serve me up like that. You know he's already declined twice, Perry. What am I supposed to do?"

"Work your usual miracle. You'll figure it out, you always do." He flashed her a semi-genuine smile, and his words sounded a little bit like a compliment.

She snorted and folded her arms across her chest, examining him closely, looking for the catch. "I guess I'll have to now that you practically promised them."

"You could have told them no," he said, watching her and raising an eyebrow when she didn't answer. He nodded his head as if he'd made his point. "And *that* is why you're on the short list for the program, Kelsey. You do whatever it takes to get the guest what they want. You don't apologize for being a shark in a shark tank. Now, go do what you do."

Again the unease of asking Micah Holmes crept back in. He seemed like a nice guy, a little bit on the quiet side with a hint of the shyness that kept him holed up in his room for five days. He probably had a very good reason for saying no.

Was he a guy who would help her out if she asked really nicely? Not a clue. Sure, they'd bonded over the box of spilled sex toys but that didn't mean he'd do a favor for her. It would take some time to get to know him better, to build on their acquaintance, before she could find the right angle to approach him with the request.

And there was the spark of attraction between them, a mutual interest.

She wouldn't stoop to sleeping with a guy to get Babette what she wanted—she drew the line at outright sexual favors—but it didn't hurt that he liked her. Everyone flirted a little to get what they needed—a big smile for the bouncer to get into the club, teasing banter with the guy at the airport to get the free seat upgrade. It was harmless. This would be no different.

Her earpiece buzzed, and she answered it. "This is Kelsey Kyle."

She was surprised to hear Micah's voice on the line. "Hi… this is Micah…Mr. Holmes…in the Executive Suite."

"Yes, Mr. Holmes. What can I do for you?" She looked at Perry, who was listening intently from the desk.

"I was wondering…" He cleared his throat and his voice took on that southern, whiskey-laced, gravel edge that made her shiver. She turned away from Perry, very aware of him staring her down, and she didn't want him to see her reaction to this guest. It was bad enough that her voice sounded breathy and shaky to her own ears. Damn, but that southern drawl made her heart pound. "I wanted to talk to you about some things for this week, and I was wondering if you have time to come back to my room."

"Yes, of course. I can come right up. Is there anything else I can do for you? Anything you need?"

A long bout of silence followed; so long she wondered if he'd hung up until she heard whispering in the background. A muffled murmur and Micah's sharp "shut up" made her curious about whom he had in his room.

She hoped to God it wasn't a hooker.

Kelsey had no desire to go to his suite and find some chick ordered off one of the many flyers they handed out on the Strip. Micah didn't strike her as the call girl type, but most of the time the guys who rented girls by the hour didn't look like the type, which was why they usually got away with it. In Vegas, nothing and no one was what they seemed, but she didn't want her bubble burst when it came to Micah Holmes, because today when he'd been down on the floor helping her corral sex toys, he'd appeared to be the sexy, honest, open kind of man who wrote books that made her cry and wish that the fiction could be reality.

His voice was louder when he spoke, like he had to force it out before he lost his nerve. "Towels. I'd like more towels, please."

"Certainly, Mr. Holmes. I'll be up in about twenty minutes."

She clicked off the call and stared at the photograph of the Vegas Strip on the wall, the Masquerade front and center.

"That was Micah Holmes," she told Perry, in case he hadn't figured it out.

"My mother was a religious woman, and she'd call that a

sign," Perry said behind her.

"My mother wasn't, and she would have said it was kismet," Kelsey murmured, more to herself than to anyone else. She weighed her options, balancing her squeamishness at trying to convince Micah and what she had to lose. She knew what she had to do.

If you grew up in Vegas, you knew that Lady Luck didn't show up very often, but when she did, you didn't ignore her. You closed your eyes, kissed the dice, and rolled for the jackpot.

And everyone knew that when you were born within the city limits of Las Vegas, gambling was in your blood.

Chapter Four

"Allen, you need to leave before she gets here," Micah said.

He moved around the room trying to organize his piles into neater piles and make the suite look more like a VIP hotel room and less like a frat house after Greek Week.

"No way. Not even your highly-trained Marine ass could get me out of here with anything less than a whole bunch of your brigades or regiments or whatever." Allen waved him off as he tried to shove a box into the overfull trash can.

"I was in a platoon, you moron." Micah lifted the couch cushions to make sure there weren't any unpleasant surprises under there. The room wasn't dirty, but he wasn't very good at picking up after himself when he was in full-on writing mode. He glanced around the room and determined that it was as good as it was going to get when the doorbell to the suite rang. He pointed at Allen as he walked over to the door. "You say hello and then you leave."

"Sure. Whatever." His best friend's agreement was

completely refuted by the shit-eating tilt of his grin. This was not going to go well.

He opened the door and found Kelsey standing on the threshold, peeking over several plush white towels stacked in her arms. Her eyes met his, and he felt a jolt of heat along his skin, in his groin. He sucked in a breath and steadied his reaction, watching her cheeks flush with her own response to him, but she didn't look away. Good. He hadn't imagined the attraction from earlier.

He took his time to take in her appearance—long, sexy legs, full breasts, her long fall of dark hair, and her light mocha skin. She was still dressed in her uniform of black, fitted suit and was still gorgeous. Gorgeous enough to make him stumble over his words a little. "Kelsey...um...you look..."

"Let her in," Allen said, and Micah gritted his teeth. He flashed a "shut up" glare at him before he pulled his head out of his ass and fell back on the manners instilled in him by his mom and finely-tuned by the U.S. Military.

"Come in, please. Thanks so much for coming up. I really appreciate it."

"It's not a problem at all." She smiled at him; it was warm and did a lot to loosen the tension in his body. He felt like he was in high school again, all false starts and insecurity around someone he was interested in. She looked over his shoulder and nodded at Allen. "Good evening."

"This is my agent and friend, Allen George," he said. "Allen, this is Kelsey Kyle, a junior concierge here at the hotel and the one assigned to me for the convention."

Allen was as smooth as ever and walked over to extend his hand to her. "Nice to meet you. I really appreciate you helping Micah out. His regular PA just left to be a full-time mom, and we had no time to get a replacement."

"It's no problem at all. I'm looking forward to it," Kelsey replied.

Allen smiled and then slid a look at him, and Micah knew he wasn't going to like what came next. He moved toward his friend, prepared to chokehold him until he passed out if necessary, but he was too late.

"Micah, she is as beautiful as you said." He grinned the grin of the truly evil and kept talking. "I totally support your plan to ask her out on a date."

For a split second, time actually stopped for the sole purpose of letting that piece of information hover in the air between them, long enough for him to plot the slow, painful death of his best friend.

Kelsey's gaze whipped back to Micah, but he couldn't tell if the new blush and half-smile was because she was embarrassed or pleased by the news he had a crush. Allen dropped that little grenade right in the middle of the room and then grabbed his coat off the back of the chair, clearly intending to leave him there to deal with whatever fallout ensued.

Bastard.

Allen held his card out to Kelsey who took it. "My contact information is on there in case you need something from me."

"Thank you. It was nice to meet you." Kelsey bobbed her head at him and then turned toward the bathroom with a nod toward Micah. "I'll go and put these towels away for you."

Micah watched her go, making sure she was out of earshot before he turned back to Allen.

"Thanks a lot, dickhead."

"Look, I knew you'd take forever to put it out there, so I saved you the trip. She knows you think she's cute. The way she was looking at you, I think it's mutual. Turn on that southern charm that all the girls fall for, and I've seen you use on rare occasions, and get the girl for once."

Micah stared at him, pissed that his little speech had seeped out a good part of his anger. Allen might be a douchebag sometimes, but he meant well, and he had just cut to the chase in a way that eliminated any way for him to chicken out.

"I'd say thank you, but part of me still wants to punch you in the face," he finally said as he pointed to the door. "Go. Get me an offer on my thriller."

Allen laughed and opened the door, yelling "you're welcome" before the door shut behind him. He raked his hands through his hair, yanking on it in frustration, and turned around to find Kelsey staring at him with a smooth expression on her face that probably served her well when dealing with crazy, grouchy, demanding hotel guests, but she couldn't hide the spark of curiosity in her eyes.

"So…" he said, lowering his hands and shoving them in his pockets for the lack of knowing what else to do with them. He was not a people person, and it only got worse when he was interested in a woman. Being with Becky had given him no experience in the dating department. That's what happened when a guy married his elementary school sweetheart two weeks after high school graduation and two weeks before boot camp.

"I placed the towels on top of the others in the bathroom," she said, jabbing her thumb at the door behind her. "You have quite a collection of them in there."

"Yeah, I do." He liked to have fresh towels, but the hotel had been so amazing at remembering his preference that he couldn't use them fast enough even with a shower when he woke up and one after his workout. It was habit he'd developed after he'd returned home from his deployment, and a simple thing like a clean towel felt like the world's best luxury. He'd meant to clear some of them out before she arrived, but he'd run out of time. Now he looked like a freak with a towel fetish. That was worse than the truth so he confessed. "I knew that. I asked for more towels so that if you got up here and I flaked out on asking you out, I'd have a good excuse."

He rushed out the last sentence, forcing himself to take the plunge. Something told him Kelsey might be worth it, so he ignored the painful twist in his stomach and went for broke. "I'm really terrible at this, but you're the most gorgeous woman I think I've ever seen. I'd really like to take you to dinner and get to know you better."

"Oh." She closed her mouth, breaking eye contact for a moment to look around the room for her answer in the artwork or the skyline just outside the windows. When she looked back at him, her expression was torn, regretful, and he knew what her answer would be. "The hotel doesn't allow us to date guests. I'm sorry."

He tried his best to hide the disappointment that shoved his guts down in his toes, but he knew he did a terrible job at it. Micah was no poker player. "Well, the last thing I want to do is get you in trouble at work. No worries," he said, waiting for her to make her excuses and leave.

"It's not that I don't think you're hot or anything or that I wouldn't love to go out to dinner with you." She paused and bit her bottom lip, the sigh that passed her lips telling him that she regretted saying no. "I just can't."

The pit eased up in his gut. She thought he was hot? He wasn't being blown off. And even though the answer wasn't what he wanted, if that was the only obstacle, he could work with it.

And…she didn't move, she stood there staring at him with a million things passing through her eyes: regret, calculation, decision, and then indecision. She was thinking really hard about this, and it gave him confidence that maybe he could change her answer.

"How about if it wasn't a date?" he asked, surprising himself with the turn this had taken. Taking the steps necessary to put himself right in front of her, he looked down at her and smiled. "What if I had a way for us to have dinner, and it wouldn't violate the rules of your job?"

She cocked her head at him, resting her hands on her hips. "What did you have in mind?"

"As a VIP guest of the hotel, I get a free excursion, and instead of hiking the desert I want to go out and have dinner and see the sights of Las Vegas." He looked at his watch. "But my personal concierge went off the clock, so unless the guy at the desk can arrange it for me at such late notice, I will be an unhappy guest."

She stared at him, the smile tugging at her lips almost breaking through. But it was her eyes that got him, sparkling with mischief and enjoying the challenge. "It *is* against Masquerade policy to have any unhappy guests."

He took a step closer and she didn't move away. They were close enough now that their arms brushed against each other, and tender jolts of electricity raced over his skin. Micah leaned down even further to account for the difference in their height, so close that he felt the warm whoosh of her exhale as she reacted to his proximity.

Chemistry. He wrote about it enough to know that they had it.

"If I have to stay here and eat room service all by myself again, I will be an unhappy guest."

She swallowed hard, her arms uncrossing and dropping to her sides. Micah took advantage and reached out to brush his fingertips against the curve of her elbow and watched as her lips parted and her pupils dilated at the caress. He could lean down and kiss her right now, and she'd probably let him. Jesus.

"Then I have no choice but to arrange for the best local guide I can find," she whispered.

"Is he or she reliable?"

"She's a local. Very reliable. She'll take you away from the Strip, let you check out a local's place."

"She sounds perfect," he said, enjoying this moment with her. This was the kind of stuff his heroes said, but he never quite pulled off in real life. With Kelsey it didn't feel forced or stupid or like he was playing a part. It felt real. "How do I get word to her?"

"She'll meet you around the corner in front of the wax museum in a half hour. She has a red Jeep." Kelsey backed up slowly, walking past him as she headed toward the door. Micah swiveled on his feet, watching the way the dark fall of her hair swayed in mesmerizing tandem with the rock of her hips. Whether she was coming or going, everything about her made him want. She gave him one last smile over her shoulder as she opened the door. "I hope you're hungry."

He took a deep breath, trying not to read too much into her comment but acknowledging the sexy, teasing timbre to her words. No matter how she intended it, his body reacted like a man denied water after too long in the desert. Muscles tight, cock half hard, heart beating like a drum. There was no denying his meaning when he answered.

"I'm starving."

Chapter Five

What the hell was she doing?

Kelsey looked across the table at Micah enjoying the food piled on his plate. She'd changed her clothes, shedding the fitted black suit of her uniform for a pair of black short-shorts, tank top, and a pair of high heel wedge sandals that made her legs look amazing. The fact that she gave a shit about how her legs looked sent all kinds of warning flares off in her head, but she closed her eyes and ignored them.

Yes, this was the perfect opportunity to get to know him better, to figure out what angle she needed to use to get him to agree to hang out with Babette, but it wasn't the only reason she'd accepted his invite. She *wanted* to go out to dinner with him. Hell, she'd wanted him to kiss her back in his room, and that was crazy. The line between her job, her status as a fangirl of Micah Holmes the author, and her fascination with Micah the man was quickly getting blurry, and she couldn't blame it on the one beer she was still sipping with dinner.

"This is amazing," Micah said as he turned to watch the chef prepare another patron's meal on the huge, circular grill in the middle of the restaurant. Diners went up to the long bar of ingredients—veggies, meat, noodles, seafood—piled it all in their bowls, topped it off with their own combination of the various oils, sauces, and spices, and handed the entire thing over to the chef, who stir-fried the meal right in front of them. "I've never been to a place like this before."

"There are a couple of these closer to the Strip, but this is the one I've gone to with my family since I was a kid. My parents know the owners, and the food is always great," she replied, watching him as he maneuvered a long noodle on his chopsticks and into his mouth. He was only succeeding about half of the time. At this rate he might starve. She giggled. "Do you want a set of cheater chopsticks? They have them for kids."

He lifted his head slowly, eyes narrowed. "You're not funny."

"And watching you waste away while you try to use those chopsticks physically hurts me." She caught the eye of the waitress and mimed her request for utensils before turning back to Micah. "How do you not know how to use chopsticks?"

"I've never been able to get the hang of it. I can take my rifle apart and put it back together faster than any guy in my platoon, but I'm all thumbs when it comes to chopsticks."

He looked up in obvious relief when the waitress arrived and placed a pile of silverware on the table. Kelsey picked up a fork and waved it in front of him, whipping it out of reach when he reached for it. She laughed at him, and Micah grabbed her wrist to claim the utensil, his warm fingers clutching her bare skin firmly but gently.

They locked eyes across the table, and the laughter continued but there was heat behind it now and she squirmed at the warmth in her belly. She licked her lips, noticing how his eyes immediately zeroed in on her movement.

Micah might think he's not that good at this, but he was doing fine in her book. If he did it any "finer," she was going to self-combust and jump him.

He appeared to be perfect, and she knew that wasn't true. Men always had an angle, and the key was to figure it out before they got in your pants. She didn't mind getting used while she was getting fucked, as long as she had full disclosure. Which probably meant she should come clean with Micah, but she knew that that much honesty at this point would ruin her efforts; her gut told her he wasn't the kind of guy who appreciated games. He was a nice guy, and suddenly she felt a little sleazy.

She tugged on her arm and he let it go, letting his fingers slide over the sensitive skin on the inside of her wrist before traveling across her palm to take possession of the fork. He lifted his lip in a sexy half-smile and turned his attention back to his plate.

She needed to get this non-date back on track even though it was the most successful date of any kind she'd had in a long while. The request from Saul was hanging over her head, and she felt weird flirting when she was hoping to get him to agree to the request.

"You grew up in Las Vegas?" he asked, pausing as he wolfed down his food. "What was that like?"

"Well, my favorite classes were 'Casino 101' and 'Showgirl Dancing,' but I think it was probably like growing up anywhere else after we worked our shift at the blackjack tables."

"I might *sound* like a country hick, but even I'm not falling for that."

She laughed and popped a shrimp in her mouth before she continued. "I loved growing up here. The Strip is only a small part of what this place is about."

"A huge part."

"A monstrously huge part and the backbone of our economy, but when you get outside of the lights it's just regular houses and schools and grocery stores." She took a sip of her beer. "My dad works for the Nevada Gaming Control Board in the Audit Division, and my mom was a librarian."

"Was it only the three of you?"

"Yep. My dad still lives in the same house where I grew up." She waited for him to ask the usual question about her mom and she saw it on his lips, but his eyes merely examined her face and then he nodded, giving her a pass. She sighed with relief because she didn't want to get into the situation with her mom; it was difficult to discuss with her friends, much less a relative stranger who'd be gone as soon as Sunday checkout came around. "From your accent and your bio, I know you grew up in Virginia."

He nodded and smiled, his eyes warm with the memory and tinged with an edge of longing. Micah Holmes was homesick. She'd bet money on it.

"A little town called Bridger Gap. We have two stoplights, the nearest mall is an hour away, and the only thing to do on Friday nights is to go to the football games and then take your girlfriend to the Tasty Freeze to cool off and to the top of Bridger Ridge to heat things up."

He waggled his eyebrows at the last bit, and she rolled her eyes. He was cute. Really sexy under all the boyish charm and goofy swagger.

"Funny. Do you still live there? I can't imagine living in such a small place."

"I do live there, and it *can* be a little claustrophobic." He put down his fork and pushed his plate out of the way, making room to lean on the table and spread his hands out. She was aware of how close their fingertips were, the whisper of a touch with each of his movements. "I was so excited to leave when I graduated. I joined the Marines before graduation and left soon after and went straight to boot camp."

She noticed that he left out the part where he got married in between and the injury that ended his military career, and wondered if he would talk about any of it. Yes, she'd read articles on all of it, but he always refused to talk about any of the details, so it was all speculation on the part of the writer. As the silence drew out, she realized he wasn't going to offer, and she didn't feel comfortable asking. Kelsey decided to keep to a safer topic. "So why go back if it feels claustrophobic?"

He shrugged, his index finger brushing against the tablecloth and occasionally along the edge of her hand. His gaze was direct; the dark brown depths warm with obvious desire. She knew she should look away but she couldn't. She liked him, especially when he looked at her like that.

"It's my home. I spent a lot of time in the desert wishing I were in the mountains, so I went back when I was discharged. I didn't have anywhere else to go," he said, breaking eye contact to look down at the table. His voice when he spoke had lost the humor for the first time since she'd known him. "I've realized it's not a good idea to move back to your hometown when your ex-wife lives there with her new husband, who just happens to be your buddy from high school." He looked up again suddenly, the brown of his gaze murkier than before. "I spend a lot of time traveling around, but I keep a small house on the mountain."

"Ouch," she whispered, not sure what to say beyond that. Kelsey found herself reaching out, her fingers brushing over his with a touch so light she might have imagined it except for the spark that zinged between them. She pulled back, reminding herself that this couldn't go anywhere. "Makes me wonder why you write the books you write."

Micah's hand chased hers on its retreat, his skin warm against hers. When his large hand wrapped around hers, she didn't pull away even though she knew she should.

"You never heard this story?" When she shook her head, he laughed and wiped his free hand over his face, his smile wide and open once again. "It's insane. I was attending Virginia Tech on the GI Bill and needed cash to pay some extra bills, and my creative writing professor gave me a flyer from my publisher looking for people to ghostwrite for them. I applied, and the romance novels offered the biggest payout. I wrote four for them before the first one hit the NYT list, and everything went nuts. Someone at the house outed me to some book bloggers, and suddenly I was the next Nicholas Sparks."

"Wow. That's amazing."

"That's one thing to call it." He pulled back and shifted in his chair, his shoulders slumped. Gone was the boyish, laid-back Micah, and here was a guy who looked about ten years older who showed the wear and tear of life. "My dream was to be the next Tom Clancy, and I'm stuck writing books about single mother ranchers and ex-con foremen who show up when she needs a good harvest to save the farm."

"You want to write about Jack Ryan and nuclear weapons?" She was interested in hearing his answer. She could never spin out stories that made her stay up all night, and she was fascinated by this part of the whole thing.

"Yep. I want to write books about spies and terrorists and the guy who never falls in love but bangs more chicks than James Bond."

"That's a lot of testosterone there."

He held out his hands in a "what can I say" gesture. "I've got a penis. It comes with the equipment."

She shook her head, not understanding what she was hearing. "If that's how you feel, how can you write those amazing, romantic stories that make everyone cry like a baby?"

"It's fiction. I'm a good storyteller, and I was in love once before. There are some experiences you never forget, and falling in love is one of them," he said. "And what I write is only about the beginning, the good stuff. I don't have to worry about what comes after. That's the part where it all falls apart. As long as I can remember how I felt in the free fall before the crash, I'm good."

That was an opening to ask about his divorce, but the flash of pain in the dark expanse of his eyes dried up the words on her tongue. It probably wasn't first non-date conversation anyway.

"What other experiences do you never forget?"

"Holding a new baby. Burying a parent. Taking a life." He moved back in and leaned across the table, and she mimicked his movement. "You've been in love before, right?"

She blinked, unprepared to have the tables turned on her. Kelsey admitted the truth before she thought too hard about it. "I thought I was."

"You *thought* you were?"

"Let's just say that working at hotel and casino in Vegas gives me lots of access to guys who remove their wedding bands the minute they get on the plane. It took me a while to realize that if their mouths are moving, then they are probably lying. I got my heart broken a time or two before I figured it out."

"Now it's my turn to say ouch."

"Yes, well. Some people are assholes and that is a good lesson to learn if you want to keep working here in Sin City." She chuckled and took another sip of beer. "I don't date, but I love my job and it takes up most of my time. I can't imagine doing anything else."

"What do you love about it?"

That was easy. "The problem-solving. The organizing. I like arranging the perfect experience for a guest and delivering it to them. If they can sit back, relax, and everything goes smoothly, I'm happy."

Micah looked around the restaurant and then winked. "You're very good at it. This is a great place, and I really needed to get out of the hotel."

"Yes, you did. The staff calls you the Hobbit because you never leave the 'Shire.'"

"I went to the gym every day," he said while laughing and shrugging in acceptance of the nickname. "I *was* working. I had an excuse."

"Well, you'll get plenty of time to meet the masses at the convention. I talked to the organizers, and you are very popular." Kelsey watched him closely, trying to gauge his potential to agree to her request. "Your fan club event tomorrow is completely sold out, and many of them would love more time to spend with you."

It wasn't a lie. Babette was not the only guest who'd asked the hotel and the convention organizers to try and arrange their own fan experience or to try and figure out where Micah was going to be so they could "accidentally" bump into him.

Now he looked uncomfortable, the kind of unease that was way down in the bones.

"I'm not good with strangers. I'm an introvert, always have been. I think it's why I was always writing stuff down. The people in my head were easier to deal with."

"But you played sports." She thought back to the bios she'd read about him over the years. "You joined the Marines, that's thousands of strangers."

"I'm better when I can blend in with the crowd. Put a uniform on me and I can disappear for a while and do my job. I was an excellent Marine because of it, I think," he said, his mouth doing that half-smile he did when he was embarrassed. She was starting to recognize his quirks and they made her heart rate kick up. "I'm better with one-on-one after I get to know someone."

"Well, you did fine with me. I had a great time." She paused, and Micah took it as the signal to get the check.

He insisted on paying for his "excursion" and she let him, also letting him pull her chair out for her and place his hand on the small of her back as he led her out of the restaurant. It was warm and heavy there, his long fingers spanning most of her body. It was also kind of old-fashioned and not something her usual dates would do. Chivalry was not alive and well in Vegas.

Kelsey knew in her gut that this superfan thing was probably dead in the water. Micah wasn't putting on false modesty or faking his bashfulness. She could tell by every awkward squirm and the way he tore his napkin into tiny little pieces that his aversion to the social aspect of his job was real. Should she even bother asking? Babette was coming to the fan club event tomorrow, and maybe the solution was to introduce them and let Micah see whom he'd be hanging out with. It might work.

They stepped out into the parking lot of the restaurant in front of a couple of cabs waiting for fares from the club next door. The music was hard to hear, but the thudding techno beat shook the pavement a little under their feet.

Micah stood close to her; his head dipped to look her in the eye. Kelsey felt the urge to lean into him, wanted to feel the solidity of the muscles she could see outlined under his shirt and jeans, and it must have shown in her eyes because he shuffled forward until their thighs and chests brushed against each other. She sucked in a soft inhale when the tips of her breasts tightened at the contact.

It had been a very long time since she'd stood so close to such a hot guy and even longer since she had found one she actually liked. Micah Holmes might not think he was like the heroes in his book, but he was pretty damn close.

"I don't know if this is appropriate for me to say on a non-date excursion, but you look gorgeous tonight," he said, flicking his gaze down to look at her sandals. "Especially your legs in those shoes. They almost made my heart stop."

She did a mental fist pump that she'd chosen the heels over the flats, but she tried to play it cool and as professional as she could be while wearing short-shorts. "Thanks for coming. I had a good time."

"I did too." He paused, and she knew what he was going to ask and her stomach sank. "I'd like to do it again."

She wanted to say yes. For the first time in a long time, she hated the no fraternization rule because she might want to take a chance on Micah Holmes. Kelsey didn't delude herself that it would be anything more than a vacation fling, but she'd bet money that he'd leave her with only good memories for a souvenir.

"I don't think that's a good idea. I really can't date guests, it's against the rules," Kelsey said, feeling in her gut how much she wished she could say something different.

"I wasn't asking for a *date*." He smiled, and the best way to describe his expression was…wicked. Micah was already crazy sexy with a sweet edge, but when his potential to be devilish was added in, her heart started pounding. "I'd like to do another non-date excursion, unless you think it's too risky."

"Of course it's risky. What if someone saw us?" The words were bitter on her tongue but they needed to be said. Tonight was dicey enough without blurring the lines between their professional relationship and what could happen between them on an up-close-and-personal basis. Even explaining that she was doing this to get another guest their request probably wouldn't be enough to save her job. "I don't think it's a good idea. I'm sorry."

He watched her closely, his fingers brushing against her

hip in a slow back-and-forth motion that made her shift and squirm in a really good way. This was tough, but even if the hotel rules weren't there, she still had the request from Saul and Babette hanging over her head, and keeping it to herself made her feel like she was being less than honest with him. She needed to keep her quest to get him to agree to the Ultimate Fan thing on the clock.

In a surprise move, Micah's fingers wrapped around her wrist and tugged her close enough for them to be pressed from top to bottom. It felt good, really amazing in a way she hadn't felt in a long time, except when she read one of his books or one of the dozens of other romance novels that filled up her ereader. The devilish tilt of his mouth was back, and there was determination in the set of his jaw. She knew she should put some distance between them because the tumble of heat in her belly told her that she was in big trouble.

"I could be a dick and check out of the hotel," he murmured, chuckling when she choked and raised her eyebrow at him in shock. "But that might make it worse for you, and I'm not that guy." Micah leaned in closer, brushing his lips against her cheek in an almost-kiss as he whispered, "I'm not good enough at this to play games, Kelsey. I think you're beautiful. I want you. I like what I know of you and I want to learn more, but I get that you are in a tough spot. So, you let me know how and when we can do this, and I'm there. Your rules."

She sucked in a breath and turned her face toward him before she thought about it. Their lips brushed against each other, a whisper of a touch, and they both froze. She held her breath, waiting to see what he would do. It would make it easier for her, his taking the lead and giving her the mental out that this wasn't on her. It was a game, a way for her play with the rules, and ignore the voice in the back of her head telling her that she needed to be straight with him about

Babette's request.

"Damn," he said on a groan and angled his head to press a hard kiss against her mouth. It was chaste for a moment, and then his tongue swept across her bottom lip and she opened to him. He held back, delving in just enough for her to taste him, to love the wet slide of their mouths against each other. The kiss had her leaning into it, fighting the desire to take it further. But she never got the chance because Micah ended it, his hand still gripping her wrist right above where her pulse pounded like a hyperactive drum. His brown eyes locked on hers for a split second before he blinked and let her go.

He stepped away from her and raised his arm to signal a nearby cab, and then leaned down to give the driver the name of the hotel through the open window. He opened the passenger door, stopping his departure when she touched his other arm. Kelsey waited until he looked down at her to speak.

"I'm not sure I believe you when you say you aren't good at this," she stuttered out, finding it difficult to catch her breath. "Because that was pretty damn good."

"I guess I haven't been properly motivated before," he said, pausing to reach and run his fingers down her arm. "I'll see you tomorrow, Kelsey. Thank you for tonight."

Chapter Six

"I have something for you, Sarina," Kelsey said, waving an envelope as she walked across the floor of her best friend's porn store.

Sarina's business, Sizzle and Pop, was as classy as an adult book, movie, and sex toy store could be. She'd taken the end storefront in a strip mall not far from the Strip surrounded by restaurants, a nail salon, and a bar on the opposite end. The space looked like a high-end department store with glass and chrome and dark built-in cabinets, spanning the vibe between masculine and feminine. She'd wanted a place that both men and women would be comfortable shopping in, and she'd succeeded.

"I hope that's my money," Sarina answered, leaning on the counter at the front of the store. Her friend was a tall, willowy redhead with green eyes that gave away her wicked sense of humor. As a foster kid growing up, she'd won a scholarship to the University of Nevada and never hesitated to apply for the small business loan she needed to open her own store. "It better be my money because we both know that sex sells, and I can't afford to just give it away."

Kelsey handed over the envelope with the check with a flourish. "Love You Big Time sends their thanks and a little something extra for giving up so much of your stock to help them out."

She watched as Sarina lifted the envelope flap and peeked inside. Her eyebrows rose, and she whistled, long and loudly.

"That will help pay for my upgraded security system." Kelsey watched her as she tapped a few keys on the cash register, opened the drawer, and slid the envelope inside. "The nail salon got hit again last night."

Oh hell. The strip mall had been experiencing a rash of crime lately: break-ins after hours, shoplifting, and robberies of patrons in the parking lot.

"Really? During or after hours?"

"After, thank God. It might give Mrs. Kim a heart attack if they robbed her while she was there." Sarina reached for a box of lubricant and began placing price stickers on the bottom. "We're all talking about getting private security in here, but you know I can't afford that. I'm barely out of my first year in business, and while I made money, Vegas isn't cheap and that might cripple me."

"What do the cops say?" Crime was a problem in town just like any place with a million people streaming through it, but the police were usually on top of it. The city couldn't have tourists afraid to come on a vacation and get robbed anywhere but at the casino.

"They say it's a new gang or something wanting to stake their claim, and they are stepping up patrols and set up some kind of sting operation." She sighed, and the look on her face was anything but confident. "I need it to stop because I'm bleeding from the thefts. I have a small margin, you know."

She did. Kelsey and Sarina had spent hours poring over her business plan and the numbers. She could take some hits, but not a monthly donation to local band of mob-connected thieves, private security, *and* an upgraded security system. Not for the long-term anyway.

"Yeah, I do."

The doorbell chimed and a customer entered the store, and Sarina smiled and told him the specials and invited him to ask if he needed help finding anything.

"I should probably go. I need to get to work," Kelsey said, looking at her watch. Today was the fan event for Micah, and she had lots to do for him, and she still had to get ready for the convention the next day.

"We came by your place last night to see if you wanted pizza, but you weren't there and you didn't answer your phone," Sarina said, her question implied.

She lived in the same condo complex with Kelsey, and the "we" she mentioned consisted of their other best friends, Aiden MacAuley and Lilah Park. They hung out four to five nights per week, and Wednesday night had evolved into pizza night for the group. Lilah said they needed to move toward having pizza night with people they also traded orgasms with, and Kelsey couldn't find any reason to disagree with that goal, except that finding that person was harder than it looked.

"I took a guest out for dinner," she said. "To the Mongolian Barbecue."

Sarina stopped her task with the bottle of lube hovering in the air. "A guest?"

"Yeah."

"Was it a Masquerade Hotel function?"

"Nope." Kelsey reached out and picked up a bottle, placing the sticker on the bottom. It gave her something to do while Sarina looked at her like she'd lost her damn mind. "It wasn't."

"That could get you fired." She put the bottle down and leaned her hip against the counter, arms crossed over her chest. "You're not stupid, so I'm waiting for the explanation that tells me you didn't hit your head." She didn't even wait for Kelsey to answer before she barreled forward. "Who was this guest?"

"Micah Holmes."

Sarina laughed. "The author? The geeky looking guy who writes those books you go all mushy over?"

She put her hand up to stop the flow of ridicule. It was an old argument between the two of them. "He's not geeky looking, those glasses are hot."

"Not my type." Sarina waved her off. "Not the point at all. Why would you take a guest out to dinner? Can't he find his own dates? It's Vegas, he's loaded, and there are women on speed dial day and night."

"He's not the hooker type, and *that* is beside the point," she said.

"Well, then what is the point?"

"I have a VIP high roller who wants his sixteenth bride to have a superfan moment with Mr. Holmes, and if I can arrange it, he'll give me the recommendation I need for the management program."

Sarina nodded, her shoulders relaxing. "So, you took out the sexy professor to get him to agree to the superfan thing. That sounds like business to me and not something that can get your ass fired. Good job."

Ouch. If it was only that straightforward.

"Not quite." Kelsey laid it all out there, hoping that her friend would see it with a better spin or have a brilliant solution. "He likes me."

"What?" Sarina wrinkled her nose at her, eyes narrow with disbelief. "So, you used the fact that he likes you to get him to agree to the superfan thing? I know you've capitalized on someone's attraction before, but going out with them is pretty cold."

"I know. I feel really shitty about it." She leaned both elbows on the countertop and put her face in her hands. This was already confusing. "It's not completely mercenary. I like him, too." She took a deep breath, "He kissed me."

"Did you kiss him back?"

She nodded. "I did."

It wasn't much of a kiss, to be honest, but it had rocked her world for those few seconds, and she'd spent the rest of the night with the weight of his mouth on hers, the taste of his tongue on her lips.

"So when are you going to come clean and not mess up something that might have potential?" Sarina asked.

That had her popping her head up, surprised at the question. "There's *no* potential. He's a guy in Las Vegas for a few days. We both know that is never anything but a fling."

"Oh, so you think *he's* playing an angle?" Sarina asked, her features loosening up with this bit of news. You didn't look like Sarina and not get hit on by every guy who passed through Vegas. She had bruises on her heart just like Kelsey. "It's still dangerous if you get caught."

"I don't know if he's got an angle. He seems like he's a nice guy," Kelsey murmured, her gut telling her that she was right. None of her alarm bells went off with Micah, which only made her situation worse. "I don't mind jamming up a jerk, but I get the feeling that I'm the user this time and not the used."

The customer from earlier was approaching the counter and Kelsey had to go, but she looked to her friend for some last minute advice.

"What should I do, Rina?"

"I don't know, Kelsey, but I know you're not that girl. You might wheel and deal and pull rabbits out of hats, but you're not the girl who goes this far to manipulate a nice guy's feelings to satisfy the whim of some VIP asshole who's been married sixteen times. At least, I hope you're not."

"You're not telling me anything I don't already know," Kelsey said, biting back the urge to reach over and shake Sarina. She needed advice, not judgment.

"Well, then you already know what to do," Sarina said, and turned her attention to the customer.

Kelsey walked out of the store, the conversation not making her feel any better. She was stuck in a place where she was going to disappoint someone who could help her out at a critical point of her career. If she didn't get the superfan moment for Babette, it was anyone's guess if she would get the program slot. She was qualified, but she wasn't the only qualified candidate.

If she confessed and told Micah, she knew it would hurt him; he gave off the "good guy" vibe in waves, and he'd done nothing to deserve that kind of crap. And it could hurt her career progression as well. She was assigned to him for the convention, which was a huge business partner for the hotel, and if he requested someone else or if he reported that he had less than stellar performance from her, it could take her out of the running.

In truth, she didn't have many options. Tomorrow she would spend the day with Micah, get to know him, and watch him with his fans. She'd take that data and figure out a way to make this work without getting more involved.

Chapter Seven

"There are so many of them…hundreds, I think," Kelsey said as she closed the door of the huge hotel ballroom.

Micah paced in front of the table set up in the front of the room for the signing part of the fan club event. Books, piles of them, were stationed behind the large screens running behind it and the full length of the room. Hanging on the screens were huge foam-mounted posters of his book covers and the promo images from the movies. He'd made them take down the ridiculous King Kong-size headshot of himself earlier.

He couldn't stand the thought of having *him* staring at *him* the whole goddamn day. He was nervous enough as it was.

"They are lined up throughout the entire second floor lobby area and then down the stairs." Kelsey kept talking as she walked over to him, stopping his pacing progress when he caught sight of her beautiful body. She even made the austere black suit look sexy, especially when she bent over and the swell of her breasts peeked out from the top of the button-down shirt. Or when she tucked her long hair behind her ear and it exposed the curve of her neck, which he really wanted to kiss and suck and taste. He was so involved in making that dirty little mental "to-do" list that he was surprised when she stopped right in front of him. Her grin was huge and very excited and completely oblivious to the turn his mind had taken. "I'm thinking hundreds and hundreds."

Jesus. He was picturing her in bed, and she was still talking about the horde of people in the lobby.

"Your legs look sexy as hell in those heels," he said in a voice low enough that only she could hear.

She raised an eyebrow at his comment. "I tell you that you have hundreds of fans outside waiting for the chance to meet you, and you're ogling my legs?"

Micah swallowed hard, his nerves taking a beating from the battling sensations of crowd anxiety and lust. "It's either that or I go back to the restroom and throw up."

Her eyes widened on a sharp laugh. "Ogle away then, ogle away."

"Your sacrifice is much appreciated." Micah stared down at her, wishing again that he'd taken the leap and *really* kissed her last night. He'd planned to do it and even leaned in to do it, but he'd zigzagged at the end and kissed her with more restraint than he thought possible and then stepped away when everything between them urged him to take it further.

Chicken shit.

If he got her to go out with him again, he would kiss her and get her in his bed and fuck her until neither of them could move. He was dying to know how she tasted, whether she liked to be kissed strong or tender, how her hands would feel on his body, the weight of her breasts in his palms, and the silk of her hair on his skin. His body grew tight, the jeans he wore becoming uncomfortable as his dick wholeheartedly supported all of the ideas of things to do to Kelsey, if he ever got that suit off.

He hadn't felt this drawn to a woman since he'd had those first, adolescent fumblings with Becky. He loved women, and he'd been with others since the divorce, and while they'd turned him on, none of them had made him feel this way. Biological-imperative lust so you didn't die of deadly semen back up and bone-deep *want* were two different things. He *wanted* Kelsey.

He rubbed a hand over his face, the scratch of his beard rough against his palm as he looked around the room. He still couldn't figure out how he got here.

"The Q&A went okay, right?" he asked, letting out a deep breath.

"You did really great." She nudged him with her elbow, shifting to follow his gaze around the room. "You told me you weren't good at the people thing. Liar."

"I'm better with a crowd, and if you ask me a direct question I can answer it." He shrugged and shoved his hands in his pockets. He knew his shortcomings, the Marines had been excellent at helping him face his weakness and capitalize on his strengths. "I can talk about characters and story and my method for writing all day long as long as you feed me the question. Just don't expect me to come up with spontaneous, interesting conversation with total strangers."

"You did an excellent job. They were eating out of your hand." She turned and gave him the side-eye. "So, why do you want to throw up?"

He groaned. How did he explain this part of it and not look like an asshole in front of the woman he hoped to convince to give him another "excursion-non-date"?

"It's the one-on-one part that freaks me out. They hug me and ask me to sign their boobs and babies, and they tell me that they are naming their unborn child after a character in one of my books. They cry…" He rocked back on his heels, dropped his chin, and let out a long breath. "They cry a lot."

"That's amazing. It means you touched them with your writing, and they are dying for you to connect with them." Kelsey turned and poked him in the side, and he flinched away when it threatened to tickle him. "You're a nice guy, warm and funny. We have no trouble talking with each other. So, what's the real problem, and what can we do to fix it?"

Her eyes were shrewd, assessing, and he knew he wouldn't get away with some half-truth with her. Usually the publicists and his PA rolled their eyes when he balked at the PR stuff, but none of them asked why. Micah didn't know how comfortable he was with the knowledge that Kelsey wouldn't let him skate on the answer, but he liked that this girl asked in the first place.

He walked over to the wall of covers ignoring the weird looks from the two publicists sent by the convention organizers as they made last minute adjustments to the books on display on the table.

"The truth is that I don't know what to say to them, and I'm terrified I'm going to let them down. Romance is not my choice of genre, but I respect that the readers have spent their hard-earned cash to buy my books. Then they spend more money to come to things like this." He pointed at the covers. "They expect me to be like the heroes in my books, and those guys are larger-than-life *on purpose*. They do the right thing, they fuck like porn stars, and they always say the perfect thing. I write them so that even their *fuck-ups* make women fall *more* in love with them. I don't want to ruin their experience by sounding stupid because I don't have a script in front of me."

She stared at him, her lips pressed into a thin line of total disbelief.

"You can't ruin it unless you're a total asshole, and I don't think you have an asshole bone in your body."

"I do. My ex-wife was quite clear on that."

"That's a story for another day and completely off topic." She looked over his shoulder at the women stacking even more books and cut her eyes back to him. "My job is to arrange things, fix things. You trust me to fix this for you?"

He considered her offer and glanced at the closed double doors that were the only thing between him and hundreds of fans who would expect him to smile and make small talk for several hours. He'd tried every other suggestion made by his publisher, always hoping for the key to making this work. It couldn't hurt to try one more thing.

"Whatever you do, it can only be an improvement."

"Yes, I know," she said with a confident smirk that made him want to kiss her all over again. She reached out and grabbed his arm, tugging him after her. "Come on, I'll make you into a romance hero if it kills me."

Chapter Eight

THURSDAY AFTERNOON
MICAH HOLMES FAN CLUB PARTY

Micah was doing fine.

Yeah, he was still nervous, his grip on the pen in his hand was tight, and he forced his smile in each photo, but only someone who knew what his slow, feral grin really looked like would realize it. But he looked good all sexy and rumpled with his glasses and beard. He wore jeans, dark, heavy boots, and a black T-shirt that read "What doesn't kill you makes you stronger. Except for bears. Bears will kill you." He was a stylist's nightmare, but the fans ate it up.

His fans were insane. For him, about him, and some were likely just certifiable. But they stood for hours for the chance for a few minutes and a photo with him, and that alone was intimidating. She understood better what was freaking Micah out.

Kelsey stood to the side commandeering the two girls lent to the event by the convention organizers. One made sure the books were at the ready and took photos, while the other went person-by-person and jotted down key pieces of info on Post-it notes. The fan handed the note to Kelsey when they got to the table, and she teed up Micah with a softball tidbit of information about the fan or prompted them with a question for him.

So far it was working.

A woman named Angie moved to the table, her eyes huge and filling with tears as she looked down at Micah. She was a crier. He hadn't been kidding when he said that his fans cried a lot when they met him. But it wasn't true when he said he didn't handle it well; he did fine. Micah didn't leap up and grab them in a huge hug, but he did smile at them, maintain eye contact, and listen attentively as they gushed about their love for his books when they could.

Angie couldn't. She was frozen in place with a big, fat tear rolling down her cheek, and Micah threw a helpless look in her direction

"Hey, Angie." Kelsey stepped up to the lady and placed a hand on her arm. She waited in line a long time and she didn't want her to miss out on her moment. "You said your favorite book is *Love Found and Lost*, right? What's your favorite part?"

Angie blinked a couple of times and then smiled, her focus back on Micah. "I love the scene where Jonathon takes Evie out on the boat, and they get caught in the rain. He takes her back to the pier, and they end up dancing in the rain and he kisses her for the first time." She let out a big sigh. "I reread it all the time."

"I love that one, too. When he picks her up and carries her to the car is amazingly sexy, right?" Kelsey asked, ignoring the look of surprise on Micah's face. "Is there a question you want to ask Micah while we get your book?"

"Yeah." Angie was past the nerves and smiled down at

Micah. "Did you base that scene on real life?"

Micah dipped his head as he began to sign the book for her. "The girl was real. The pier and the lake are still there. The rain storm happened." He looked up and winked at Angie and ensured that if she wasn't already in love with him, she was now. "And the rest will remain my secret to protect the guilty."

Kelsey sighed a little along with Angie. Micah might think he wasn't good at this and maybe he wasn't the best, but when he got it right…he fucking got it right.

Maybe this was the solution to the superfan problem. She could offer to "third wheel" the event and help him out, run interference with Babette. It might work, and then it would be a win-win for everyone. She sighed at her crazy dream; Babette would never agree to that.

He handed over the book and then leaned in for the photo and smiled as she walked away.

"You're doing great," Kelsey leaned over to whisper in Micah's ear. He kept his head dipped down but she could see the smile on his lips and the tiny shake of his head. "You *are*."

"You're holding my hand the whole way. It's not me. I'm just good at following directions.

"Fine. You're right. This is all me. Why are you even here?" She bumped him with her shoulder. "Get out of the chair, you big loser."

He chuckled and grabbed his bottle of water, taking a drink and smiling over at her. Kelsey's breath caught on her laughter, remembering how good his mouth felt on hers, the soft brush of his beard on her skin. He locked eyes with her and stopped, his bottle hovering in midair as whatever pulsed between them surged and popped.

Damn.

"You thirsty, Kelsey?" His question was low and full of every dirty, sexy innuendo you could put in it.

Yeah. Damn.

She huffed out a quick laugh and shook her head. "I'm good. We'll take a break after the next one, and I'll get something then."

"Suit yourself."

Micah smirked, his lip lifting in a teasing, sexy shadow of his usual grin, and she cursed under breath. He tipped the bottle at her and then took another drink. She took a deep breath and turned to face the crowd once again. The next woman stepped up and all the butterflies inside were replaced by the feeling of the *Titanic* sinking in her belly.

Babette Forasch.

It shouldn't have been that much of a surprise. Babette was a huge fan and probably a member of the fan club. Hell, she was probably the President. She turned to face Babette and smiled, making introductions. "Mr. Holmes, this is Babette Forasch. Her husband is a highly valued, frequent guest of the Masquerade, and she is your biggest fan."

Her voice sounded forced even to her own ears, so she made a mental note to dial back the enthusiasm. It would not do to make him suspicious.

Micah eyed her curiously before turning to Babette with a smile as he reached for a book from the pile. "It's nice to meet you. Why don't you tell me who your favorite character is while I sign a book for you?"

Kelsey barely had a moment to give Micah a mental thumbs up for pulling up one of the tried-and-true conversation starters she'd fed him all day when Babette got out of line and sidled around to Micah's side of the table. Of course the wife of the VIP would be the one to break the rules. It made the situation not only potentially risky but also delicate from a guest relations standpoint.

Kelsey made eye contact with the security guy standing behind them, but Micah spied her movement and held them both off with a discreetly raised hand. The guard quickly assessed the situation, and while he remained where he was, his eyes were riveted on what was happening. All Kelsey could do was stand by and seethe.

Babette leaned over the table, her ample breasts lifted high and thrust so close to his face that Micah backed up a little bit. They were probably the best breasts Saul's money could buy, and it was only natural that his eyes strayed to what she had on offer. Kelsey gripped the edge of the table, keeping the sharp spike of jealousy at bay. She had no right to feel possessive over Micah; in fact, the feeling was probably due to the fact that she disliked Babette and resented her impossible request.

Babette didn't take the body language cues but leaned in even closer, her hot pink lips spread in a wide, leering smile. "My favorite character is Lucas James in *Silent Winter*."

"Really? Why is that?" Micah cleared his throat and pushed his glasses up on his nose, keeping his gaze fixated on the book he was signing.

If Babette got any closer to Micah, she'd be wearing the same shirt, but it didn't prevent Kelsey from hearing her breathy reply.

"Because he fucks his woman like he's going to die if he doesn't have her. I read those scenes and pretend I'm her." Babette giggled and traced a fingernail up Micah's arm and then played with the hem of his T-shirt sleeve. "That guy is an insatiable animal, and I wonder if you get as dirty as he does when you get a woman in bed."

Whoa. Kelsey blinked. The security guard coughed. She wished she had a rewind button so she could make sure she'd heard her right.

Micah cleared his throat, his pen poised over the book as his neck flushed red. "That's the beauty of fiction. I get to sit around and make stuff up all day."

"Well, that's a real good imagination you've got there. I'm sure you can use it in all parts of your life," Babette cooed, and Kelsey had to step in and break this up before she had to pass out barf bags. People were starting to stare, and that was not a good thing. She put on her best concierge smile and got the little nightmare moving along.

"Excellent question, Mrs. Forasch! Do you have a camera? I'd be happy to take a photo of the two of you."

Babette paused, her irritation at the interruption apparent, and Kelsey knew that this little incident would come back and bite her in the ass. Just one more reason to make sure Babette got what she wanted and didn't have any reason to hold a grudge.

Kelsey took Babette's blinged-out phone and pressed the camera icon as the two subjects of the photograph smiled and leaned into the frame.

"I'll take a couple of shots to make sure we get a good one," Kelsey said as she looked at the image on the screen. Babette looked predatory; Micah appeared nauseous but he held the pose while she took one, then two, and a third for good measure.

If she hadn't been focused on the scene, she might have missed the slide of Babette's hand over his thigh and between his legs. But she didn't. Micah jumped and banged against the bottom of the table, knocking over the stacks of books and causing his water bottle to roll off and land on the floor with a sloshy thud.

Babette laughed, her devious chuckle making her breasts jiggle as she straightened up and adjusted her short skirt.

"Thanks, Micah. I'll see you soon," she said with a not-so-subtle sly eye aimed at Kelsey.

"Thanks for coming, Mrs. Forasch," she said, placing her hand on the woman's back to steer her away from the table.

"Are you still working on my request, Kelsey?" Babette

asked, not even trying to keep her voice down. Kelsey caught the quick glance from Micah, curious but distracted by the movements of the other assistants as they righted the stack of books on the table. "I expected to hear from you by now."

Kelsey grabbed her elbow and pulled her further away. "I'm working on it, I promise you."

"I hope you can deliver on that promise." Babette's gaze was hard and assessing, and Kelsey knew she wouldn't hesitate to fuck up her career if she didn't make this happen. She wasn't surprised. You didn't get to be the wife of Saul Forasch if you weren't a woman who only played to win.

Kelsey watched her walk away, leaving behind a knot in the pit of her stomach and the harsh reality of how little wiggle room she had here.

"Fuck," she mumbled under breath, letting out a yelp of surprise when she turned and saw Micah standing behind her. He reached out to steady her, his eyes searching and his expression inquisitive.

"You okay?"

"Yeah, yeah." Kelsey pushed her hair behind her ear and made sure she smiled, leaning in as if she was sharing a secret. "She has a little bit of a crush on you."

"I noticed." He groaned and jammed his hands in his pockets, a gesture she already recognized. "She was enthusiastic."

"You're very diplomatic, Mr. Holmes."

"I'm a little bit scared of her." Now it was his turn to lean in and tell her a secret. "She tried to grab my nuts. Did you see that? I'm traumatized."

Inside she cringed at how much more difficult Babette had made her assignment, but she had to agree.

"*You* are? I had to actually look at it happening up close on the screen."

"No comparison," he insisted. "No. Comparison. At. All."

"We will have to agree to disagree."

"So what did she ask you to do? What was she talking about?" he asked and her stomach dropped into the toes of her stilettos. Shit. She hadn't thought he'd heard, and after what happened, now was not the time to introduce the idea of his spending more time with Babette.

"Just a special excursion request. Typical stuff." She shrugged as if it was nothing. "Come on," she gestured to the area behind the bank of folding screens. "Now is a great time for you to take a break."

A quick signal to the assistants and the announcement was made that Micah was taking a short break, and they scooted out of sight. Behind the screens was a storage area for boxes of books, but there was also of cooler full of bottled water. Kelsey reached in and snagged two, the cold moisture against the skin of her hand making her suck in a sharp breath at the contrast in sensation. She handed one to Micah, and they found a stack of boxes tall enough to make a perch for them the lean on.

He was close to her in the small space, his arm brushing hers as they both gulped down the cool water. Kelsey hadn't realized how thirsty she was until she took the first sip. This close she could smell his cologne, woodsy and sharp, it was warm and sexy; very much Micah.

"I feel like I've been talking for hours," she said, placing the cap back on the bottle and stretching her neck from side-to-side.

"You *have* been talking for hours," he answered, nudging her with his elbow. "Thanks for what you did out there. You helped me out so much."

She shrugged. "Years of facilitating meet and greets with guests at the hotel and I've perfected the conversational softball."

"That was major league playing out there," he answered,

his gaze landing on her face and staying there. This proximity made her nervous, her belly tightening with the effect his body heat and scent had on her. She kept her eyes glued on her shoes, trying to maintain some distance between them after last night and earlier today. He did nothing to shield his attraction, and she had no doubt that her own longing would show if he got a good look at her. "You sure know a lot about my books."

She rolled her eyes and smirked self-consciously, willing to give him this. "I've read them all. Many times."

"Really?" He dipped his head to catch her eyes, and she had to look at him. "You're a Micah Holmes fan?"

She refused to answer that question. His cocky grin pissed her off a little bit, and she didn't want to give him that satisfaction or the leverage. Besides, it could lead to conversations about her past and what her future looked like when she let her own dreams loose—dreams that belonged between the pages of books like the ones in the boxes around her because they rarely happened in real life.

Kelsey reached over and grabbed a container of brownies a fan had brought him earlier today. It lay in a pile of homemade quilts and blankets, jewelry, and other items crafted lovingly by readers who loved his books.

"Do you need a snack?" She peeled back the top, and the scent of milk chocolate made her mouth water. She reached in to snag a bar but he stopped her, his hand on her own.

"You can't eat those."

"Why not?"

"They might be crazy people brownies," he said, his expression serious as he placed the top back on the container.

She huffed out a laugh, not sure she heard him right. "Crazy people brownies?"

He smiled, and she responded with her own. His grin was contagious, sexy, hot.

"Don't get me wrong, my fans are very nice people. They mean well, but there's always a chance that one of them might be a little nuts, so you don't want to take a chance." He laughed outright, the rumble deep and rough in his chest, and she couldn't help but respond. She leaned forward, encouraging him with her body language to continue with his story. "One time Allen ate some brownies from a signing in Colorado, and they were made with pot. He was high as a fucking kite for hours."

"Okay, no brownies." Kelsey took the container from his hands and placed it back on the pile. They laughed, her own giggles making it almost impossible to take another drink without spilling.

He stared at her, his own laughter dying out first, and she knew what was coming. Her pulse sped up and she didn't know if it was because of his interest or her anxiety with her deception. In truth, it was a little of both. She wasn't cut out for all this damn intrigue when it came down to it.

"Have dinner with me tonight." He leaned in close when he growled out his plea, his breath warm against her cheek.

Kelsey shook her head once. "You know I can't."

"Yes. I do." He stayed where he was, not touching her but it felt like he was all over her. "But it's not stopping me from asking."

She looked at him then, their mouths a hair's breadth from touching, breaths mingling. Heavy breathing in tandem. His brown eyes were liquid heat, full of desire but also with his usual humor and that's what got her. Inside of all the heavy come-on was Micah…and he was damn near irresistible.

"Why can't you be like all the other guys who come to Vegas?" She heard herself ask before she knew what she was saying. If he were, this would be so much easier. The lines between sex and business would be very clear in her mind.

"I'm not?"

She gave one firm shake of her head, eyes still locked on his. "No, you're not."

That's all she was going to say because anything more would give too much away. Too much of *her* away.

"So what does this have to be to make me like all the other guys who come to Vegas? What gets you to say yes to dinner with me?"

Oh hell. She knew exactly what she'd need from him to risk taking this where he clearly wanted it to go. Why was he doing this? Why was he handing her the perfect excuse to have her cake and eat it, too? Why was he putting the temptation right in front of her?

"Come on," he said, his finger stroking the inside of her wrist where her pulse was going nuts, and making any denial of his impact on her a waste of time. "I know last night was risky, but we can be discreet. We can discuss logistics of the rest of the convention over the meal, and you can pretend it's work."

She flinched a little bit. This entire scenario already involved more work than he realized.

But he didn't stop.

"Tell me what this needs to be in order for you to say yes, and I'm okay with it." He glanced down between them for a split second, his huff of laughter sharp with an edge of self-deprecation. "You've kind of got me by the balls here, Kelsey. I want you. So I'll ask you again. What does this have to be to make me like any other guy who comes to Vegas?"

He had her by the balls, too. She could either answer his question directly or hide behind the truth that any interaction with a guest was off-limits. Micah was impatient, and he took her silence for the indecision that it was. His groan of frustration accentuated the movement of his body between her legs, as he maneuvered closer, his position forcing her to look up at him."

"Tell me. Tell me I'm reading this thing wrong between us and I'll leave you alone."

Kelsey opened her mouth to say it, to deny the desire rolling between them but it was like dust on her tongue. She swallowed hard, finding her voice and shocking herself with her response.

"No strings, nothing beyond the end of the convention. It would be temporary."

She could live with it. No promises. No emotional entanglement on either side. He could be discreet; this she knew in her bones. She could do what she needed to do with no prick to her conscience that she was leading a guy on who was emotionally invested.

Micah nodded, his lips twisting in a slight grin as he leaned forward and covered her mouth with his own. One moment it was the burble of the crowd waiting behind them and tension strung so tight it was almost a physical thing and then the next it was a long sigh and his tongue sliding inside.

He didn't touch her anywhere else, and she remained where she was, the only connection the one of lips and tongue and teeth. Kelsey tilted her head, and he took it as the invitation it was to delve deeper and to show her just how hot his passion ran.

Possession. Lust. Taking.

It was all there in his kiss and she drank him in, thirstier for his kiss than she was for the water.

He pulled back, breaking it off too soon, and her body leaned forward involuntarily to extend the kiss. His breath was still warm on her lips as he panted heavily. She opened her eyes, blinking slightly in the sudden contrast of the glare from the lights. When she could focus, all she saw were his eyes searching her own for something…

"I think we've got a deal, Kelsey Kyle."

Chapter Nine

"This is my favorite bar in all of Las Vegas," Kelsey said.

She turned to look at Micah who was standing on the sidewalk gazing up at the two story building facade with the pseudo-Manhattan skyline and a gigantic mirror ball mounted at the tip on a large pole. NYE, in huge rhinestone-covered letters, was emblazoned across the roof and backlit just in case you were blind and missed it. Without a doubt it was an outrageous sight even by Las Vegas standards.

"Is that a disco ball?" he asked, squinting against the harsh glare of the lights.

"Nope, guess again," she teased, wondering if he would figure it out. She kept watching as his gaze roamed over the entire facade until a slow smile softened the hard line of his mouth caused by his concentration.

"Is that the big ball that drops in Times Square on New Year's Eve?"

"Ding! Ding! Ding! Get that man a prize." Kelsey reached

out and looped her hand around his arm to lead him into the club. There was a line, as usual, but she'd sent so many hotel guests here that she never had to wait, and they eased past the bouncer and into the bar. "Every night in this place is New Year's Eve. Party hats and favors, live entertainment, a well-equipped bar, and the ten second countdown at midnight complete with a kiss if you have a willing partner."

He looked down at her, his eyes going dark and his drawl deepening. "For the record, I'm willing."

"For the record, you're killing me with the accent when you say stuff like that." And that was an understatement. Micah had her head spinning like a roulette wheel, and she had a feeling that any number she landed on was going to be lucky tonight. She spotted Aiden waving at her from across the room. It looked like they'd been able to secure a table. "Come on. I'll introduce you to my best friends, and we can get a drink and dance."

"I don't really dance," he said, pulling her closer as they navigated the crowd.

She laughed and shook her head, shouting a little to be heard as they pushed through the crowd. "Is that a man or Marine thing?"

"It's an 'I'm a guy who grew up in the mountains of Virginia, and we don't dance thing.'"

"Oh hell, don't be a guy. Just don't," she said, remembering her favorite movie, *Say Anything*, and improvised the line. "Don't be a guy, Micah, be a man."

He rolled his eyes and huffed a growl against her ear. "Where I come from, a man hunts, farms, breaks horses, and knows how to survive the mountain."

"Okay, so you catch the bacon and bring it home, but there's more than one appetite to feed for a woman."

She felt him smile against her earlobe, his hand sliding across her abdomen and drawing her up short in the crowd until she was flush against him. His face buried in her hair, and his strong, muscled chest resting against her back, her ass cradled against his groin. Kelsey gasped, thinking that Micah was more like the heroes in his books than he thought. This was dangerous but she couldn't help herself. She hadn't been tempted in a long time, and he was making her ache with desire.

"I can take care of whatever hunger you have, Kelsey." His breath was sharp against her neck, hot even with the press of the bodies all around them. "But you'll never see my ass on *Dancing with the Stars*."

She snickered, wondering how he could get her hot and make her laugh at the same time. It was a dangerous combination, and she needed to remember her rules to avoid the pitfalls of getting too enthralled by a man with a sexy accent and a hard body. Sex was okay. No strings. Loose. Easy.

She couldn't afford to get involved.

"Oh, man." She gripped his hand and tugged him with her as she resumed their progress across the floor of the club. "If you're going to keep talking like that, I need something cold and top shelf."

He didn't say anything, but he did keep his arm wrapped around her middle even when they stopped at one of the booths that lined the back of the room. From here there was easy access to the bar and an excellent view of the dance floor. The gang was here, all perched on their seats, devouring Micah with their eyes and not even trying to be subtle.

"Micah Holmes, these are my best friends: Aiden MacAuley, Sarina Court, and Lilah Park." She pointed out each one as she made her way around the table, and they each saluted him with their drink and a smile. "This is Micah."

"Hey, man." Aiden extended his hand and flashed his wide grin that could make anyone feel comfortable. "Glad you could make it and increase the testosterone factor tonight."

"You bet." Micah laughed, shook his hand, and then returned it to loop around her waist. She ignored the raised eyebrow from Sarina, hoping that Micah didn't catch it. "I'm just happy to get out of my hotel room for awhile. I've been cooped up there for almost a week working."

"And don't forget your trauma from earlier today," Kelsey said. "It was either dancing or therapy."

"It sounds like you need a drink," added Aiden, nodding toward the bar. "You want to go get something? I'll keep you company, and you can tell me all about your trauma."

Micah turned to her. "What do you want?"

"A beer. Whatever's on tap and not domestic," she answered, liking how he pressed a quick kiss against her hair before he took off with Aiden. It wasn't crazy sexual but the gesture got her heartbeat revved up at least a couple more RPMs.

"Okay, he is still geeky, but really fucking sexy," Sarina said as soon as the guys were out of earshot. "I completely get why you're breaking your rule for him."

"Wait? What? Breaking what rule?" Lilah asked, leaning across the table, eyes wide as she took a sip from her frozen fruity drink. Kelsey could feel her lips pucker just imagining the sugar level in her beverage; Lilah liked her alcohol to taste like Kool-Aid on crack. "Who was the hot guy?"

Sarina stepped in to explain before Kelsey could get her mouth open. "He's a VIP guest at the hotel, and she's been assigned as his personal concierge."

Lilah's hand paused in midair as she lifted her drink to her mouth. "That could get your ass fired."

"I know. I know." Kelsey leaned in close, not wanting to yell her business in the crowded club. "I have my reasons."

"Are you talking about the favor you need from him for another guest, or the fact that you want in his pants?" Sarina asked, her green eyes shrewd as they drilled into her from across the table. It was clear that she didn't approve.

Lilah lifted a hand. "Wait. I'm sensing a lot of 'tude coming off you, so what did I miss?" She turned to look at Kelsey. "What's going on with Micah?"

She explained the situation with Babette and Saul and the recommendation, and then the entire interaction with Micah. She left out nothing. There was no point in hiding stuff from her friends; both Lilah and Sarina had a bullshit detector about people that was spot on.

"So, you haven't told him about the Babette thing, but you hope to persuade him to do it for you when you butter him up enough, and you agreed to have a sorta friends-with-benefits arrangement with him so that you can get laid." Lilah cocked her head at her, the precision of her thoughts cutting through all the bullshit. "But they aren't related in your mind, and you can sleep at night because he agreed to be fuck buddies until Sunday. Did I get that right?"

Lilah was spooky smart. Brain surgeon smart, aerospace engineer smart. And she'd have been one if her life had been different, if her traditional Korean family had encouraged her to go and do something other than get married and have a family and then ditched her when she'd refused. Instead, she was managing one of the popular marriage chapels on the Strip, going to college part-time, and refusing to deal with the estranged relationship she had with her family.

But she was serious, and everything about her tone and expression told Kelsey she thought her rationale was complete and utter bullshit. In case Kelsey didn't get all the signals, she spelled it out for her.

"That's nuts, Kelsey, and it's going to backfire in your face. I don't know if it will be on the job front or on the personal side of things, but this is too interwoven for them not to create the cold-fusion equivalent of disaster for you." Lilah nodded emphatically before taking another quick sip of her drink.

"I'll keep the Ben & Jerry's stocked up for when this goes tits up."

"And I've got the perfect vibrator to use post-heartbreak. You'll love it. I can't keep it in stock," Sarina said as serious as a heart attack. Sarina never joked about sex toys. That was serious business.

"Fuck you both," Kelsey groaned, wondering why she told them anything.

Sarina held out her drink, and Kelsey accepted it gratefully and took a long swallow of whiskey on the rocks.

"Thank you for that concise depiction of the apocalypse also known as my life." She continued after the whiskey had burned its way down her throat.

"I'm not trying to be a bitch, but you're breaking the rules for this guy, and that tells me something,"

Lilah looked at Sarina for confirmation and when her friend nodded in agreement, Kelsey lost some of her patience. If they thought they held the keys to her fucked up kingdom, then she wanted to know how to get in.

"Just tell me. Please."

"If you're breaking the rules for this guy." Lilah counted them off on her fingers. "Not only breaking the no frat rule at work but agreeing to any kind of thing with a tourist, then he's got something going on that makes him different."

Sarina joined in. "Exactly. He's not just any other guy if you're doing this, and I would hate to see you pass up something potentially good because there are too many secrets and omissions to keep straight."

She could acknowledge the truth of some things they said. "Okay, you're right. He is different in the fact that I believe he'll keep it loose and easy and play by the rules. He's not a player, and I don't think he's lied to me once since I've known him. There's no woman waiting in a half-empty bed at home, and most importantly, he's going back to that home on

Sunday."

"And you just described every one of those books you love to read, every rom-com movie where the couple rides off into the sunset," Sarina said.

"And that is why they are books and movies." Kelsey cut to the chase, there were truths that they all knew well. "We all know that kind of stuff is so rare in real life that it has to be fiction. I'm not naive enough to delude myself that sex, no matter how good it is, will lead to me finding the love of my life and then ruining it because of a stupid business transaction. I'm not fucking Kate Hudson."

The silence at the table was weird in light of the club chaos around them. They all stared at each other, all of them too stubborn to break eye contact first and lose the battle of wills. It was a miracle that they didn't kill each other at times; they acted more like sisters than friends. And it was anybody's guess on any given day if they were the snuggle-under-the-covers-together sisters or the have-to-share-a-bathroom-as-a-teenager sisters. But she loved them. Yes, she did.

"Yeah, but he kind of sounds like Matthew McConaughey with that accent," Sarina offered up as a peace offering. They all laughed, the tension broken as if it had never been there and Lilah dove back into the fray.

"So, have you sampled the goods yet?"

Kelsey nodded, biting her bottom lip as she remembered the kiss from this afternoon. It wasn't over-the-top, and he really hadn't touched her but that kiss still made her belly clench in anticipation of the next one. It would be good between them, she knew. When you had chemistry like they did out of bed, chances were it transferred to action between the sheets; and they had it. In spades.

"He kissed me. Twice."

Sarina and Lilah exchanged a glance, and she could read them like a book.

She sighed heavily, knowing that she really didn't want to know. "What?"

"If you have that sappy look on your face from one kiss, I'll keep that Ben & Jerry's on standby, that's all I'm saying," Lilah said with a shrug.

"I'll put one of those vibrators in the back for you," Sarina offered up, sneaking a side-glance at Lilah that Kelsey couldn't miss. She smirked and Lilah's shoulders shook with the effort to hold in her laughter. Kelsey's grin cut loose and she threw a napkin at them, disgusted and relieved that she had friends who had her back no matter what.

"Oh, you two can kiss my ass." She turned and craned her neck toward the bar. It was crowded, but she could see the guys at the front of the pack. "I need alcohol if I'm supposed to deal with the two of you tonight."

...

"So, can you feel how much they are talking about you right now?" Aiden asked.

Micah laughed and looked over at the man causally leaning against the bar next to him. He immediately understood why Kelsey was friends with him. Aiden was about six feet tall with dark hair and blue eyes, and a quick grin and easygoing manner, but it was his voice that drew your attention. Smooth and deep, it was the kind of voice that you immediately trusted. He couldn't describe it any better than that.

"I feel like I have this burning spot on the back of my head," Micah said, raising his hand to touch the spot. He was joking but he wouldn't be surprised if it was on fire with the scrutiny aimed at him tonight. It was to be expected when a new guy showed up on the scene, and he was glad that Kelsey had such good friends.

"Ah, that would be the bull's eye of the best friends. If you screw over Kelsey, then their X-ray death glare will hit that spot and your head will explode."

"Nice to know. I'll make sure that I'm on my best behavior." Micah paused as Aiden gave the drink order to the bartender, shouting it over the social chaos. When he turned back to face him, he couldn't resist asking. "So, why are you here? Shouldn't you be back there with them?"

He shook his head. "I'm here to talk to you as a guy and see if you're a dick."

"Got it." Micah was tempted to ask him what the verdict was, but he wasn't sure he wanted to know. He also wasn't sure where Aiden fit in this equation. "Are you dating one of the girls?"

"Oh, no. See, while I'm supposed to see if you're a dick, I *like* dick." Aiden said, accepting the first of several drinks from the bartender. "So, the girls are really never going to be my type."

"That's cool," he said with a laugh. He liked Aiden, weird sense of humor and all. He took the next beverage from the staff, doing a mental check on what they were waiting on. "What do you do?"

"I'm a voiceover artist. I do commercials, documentaries." He shot Micah a smirk. "I did two of your books, dude."

"Really? Oh shit, that's embarrassing."

"No worries, man. It's not like we ever talked about the deal. My agent set it up, but I gotta tell you that the checks are amazing. You sell a shit-ton of books."

"Glad I could help you out, man." Micah reached for the last drink, pausing when Aiden nudged him with his elbow. His expression was serious but also apologetic, and Micah knew what was coming.

"I have to ask if you're a good guy. I'm not Kelsey's dad, but the guy is huge, and if you fuck her up, we'll both be on your ass."

Micah nodded, appreciating his asking. He had sisters and he did what he had to do to protect them, and that included letting the guys sniffing around know that they weren't long for this planet if they made them cry. He could only be honest.

"Per Kelsey's rules, it's just for fun and only until I'm gone on Sunday."

Aiden contemplated his answer, nodding in understanding. "Kelsey has been burned. Scorched earth with her in the emotions department so I'm not surprised, but she's not so tough underneath all of her armor. She's a strong woman, but everyone can be vulnerable to the right person. Just be careful. I don't want to have to kick your ass."

Micah couldn't resist asking. "You want to give me a clue to what happened to her? I'd be lying if I said I didn't like her. She's funny, gorgeous, smart. It's only natural."

"Oh, that's not my story to tell, but I'll caution you to keep to the rules. Kelsey doesn't deviate from her plans very often, and if you think you're going to sweep her off her feet by the weekend, you might be nursing some pain on the plane ride home."

They were jostled by people anxious to get to the bar, and by unspoken agreement they moved back toward the table, dodging dancing bodies and clusters of people. Kelsey moved to his side when he passed out the drinks, allowing him to slip his arm around her waist as they all enjoyed the coveted drinks.

"Did you get the third degree?" Kelsey asked, her breath tickling his ear.

"He wasn't so bad." Micah glanced over at where Aiden stood chatting with a group of people nearby. "He's a good friend. You're lucky."

"I really am."

"I'm pretty lucky tonight as well," he said, pressing a hot

kiss to the side of her neck. She shivered against him and he did it again, relishing her reaction.

"You keep being so sweet, and you might get even luckier." She trailed a hand down his chest, hooking her finger in the belt loop on his jeans and dragging him closer. His groin pressed against her and they both groaned a little, laughing when a passerby jostled them into the table.

He reached out to steady the drinks and noticed the laser-like focus of her two friends on everything they did. Sarina arched an eyebrow, and Lilah winked.

"How did you all meet?" Micah directed his question to include Sarina and Lilah.

"Our condo complex," Sarina said before taking a quick sip. "I bought at the same time as Aiden and Kelsey, and Lilah moved into the sublease about six months later. That was three years ago, and we've been friends ever since."

"Are you going to dance with me?" Kelsey asked, tugging on the arm looped around her waist. "Come on. I promise you'll like it."

"I told you that I don't dance," he shook his head, looking toward Sarina and Lilah for a rescue. They shook their heads, laughing when he huffed out his indignation. "You guys are going to throw me to the wolves?"

"You look like you can handle yourself," Lilah said, her eyes and smile sparkling with mischief. "Send up a flare if you need a rescue."

He gave in, not really minding any excuse to rub against Kelsey and curious to see what she looked like when she danced. She moved like sex when she was just walking around. She pulled on his hand and he stalled her, gulping down the rest of his drink before following her out onto the floor.

"I really can't dance," he murmured against her ear, catching his breath when her breasts brushed against his chest. His cock jolted in his jeans and he decided that if this was how his body would react to her movement, then he might not mind giving in this one time.

She laughed, placing his hands on her hips as she began to move her hips. They swayed to the beat of the music for half a song and then there was too much room between them, so he dug his fingers into her and pulled her as close as they could get without committing an act that would probably get them arrested.

The music ebbed and flowed between popular rock and techno crap, and all of it would have made his skin crawl if he hadn't been entirely focused on the woman in his arms. He still couldn't dance, but he could definitely remain in her orbit, allowing her to use his body as a balance or a stripper pole depending on the song and her mood.

"You lied, Micah Holmes. You can dance!" she yelled in the middle of a song with a driving beat of sex and lust. He was enjoying the feel of her body against him, really glad that the dark of the club disguised his erection from everyone but Kelsey. She ground into him, her eyes bright with mischief.

"You'll pay for that later," he growled into her ear before she playfully spun away. This Kelsey was fascinating to watch, no trace of the buttoned-up woman from the hotel. That girl was replaced with hair that was wild with her movements, miniskirt showing off miles of leg, and a tank top that left nothing to the imagination. As much as he wanted to get to the hotel and get Kelsey into his bed and peel back all those layers of reserve, he hoped that the club Kelsey would join him as well.

The girls bounced up to them, interrupting his thoughts with their laughing, drunken movements. Lilah was blitzed, her eyes closed as she undulated to music that was only playing in her head, while Sarina did the bump with Kelsey. He looked around, spotting Aiden near the back of the club with a tall, dark-haired man. They didn't look like they were having as good a time. In fact, Aiden looked like he needed ten more drinks.

"Who's that guy with Aiden?" he shouted to the girls, pointing when they craned their necks to look around the space. When they found him, all three of their faces fell and their steps faltered. Apparently he'd found the one thing that could ruin the party.

"That's his ex," Kelsey said, her nose scrunched up in dislike.

Sarina added her two cents. "He's still in the closet and wants to drag Aiden back in there with him."

"Fucker," was all Lilah added to the conversation, but he got her point.

The music cut out, and the lights went up a little as an announcer's voice railed out over the sound system as staff walked around handing out noisemakers and party hats.

"Okay, people, it's close to midnight so grab a noisemaker and someone to kiss, and get ready for the countdown."

The crowd around them went wild with shouts and catcalls, and Micah couldn't help but get sucked up into the excitement. He knew it wasn't New Year's Eve but it didn't matter, his pulse still sped up at the idea of the impending faux countdown.

He grabbed Kelsey around the waist, pleased when she came eagerly, wrapping her arms around his neck.

The announcer burst out again as a live feed of the ball outside on the roof flashed up on every screen in the place. "Okay, people we are at twenty seconds. Fifteen." His voice rose with his own excitement as everyone on the floor joined him.

Micah locked eyes with Kelsey, pulling her in closer as they counted down together, their lips only a hair's breadth apart.

"Ten. Nine. Eight. Seven. Six." He moved his hand up her

back until he cupped her neck, his fingers twisting in her hair. "Five. Four. Three. Two. One."

The ceiling opened above them, and glitter of every color and shape and size fell. It was a waterfall of sparkly plastic and proved that Vegas was the glitter capital of the world. And then he was kissing her, bold and hot as he coaxed her open so that he could taste. Possess. Take. She moaned against him, her arms wrapping tighter around him as she allowed him to dive in deeper, and she plunged in his mouth seeking her own pleasure.

Micah trailed a hand down her back, loving the play of her muscles under his hands. Everything about this moment was magnified as the roar around them became a low throb in the very far distance, and they were alone in the crowd of people. His hand cupped her ass, his fingertips finding the hot swell of her just beyond the short hem. He traced the curve, the desire to peel back her panties, the skirt, and all of her clothes was overwhelming.

He pulled away, loving the way her lips were swollen and a deep red from their kisses. He dipped in and bit her bottom lip, tugging on it with a gentle pull before releasing it again. He opened his mouth to speak, but she beat him to it. She asked him what had been on the tip of his tongue.

"Will you come home with me?"

Chapter Ten

"This place looks really familiar," Micah said.

He let go of her hand and made a complete circle in the courtyard of her condo community. In the center of the brick paved terrace was a large rectangular pool surrounded by the two-story building on three sides. The architectural design was Spanish–style villa with terra cotta walls and red tiles on the roof. She watched and waited, loving the way his grin spread when he figured it out.

"Holy shit. It's Melrose Place," he said, looking at her for confirmation.

"Yep." She nodded and laughed. "The builder was a huge Aaron Spelling fan. There's a development on the southern side of Vegas with houses that all look like they are straight from Dynasty on streets named Carrington Drive and Alexis Place."

"That's insane, and strangely I feel the need to go find them and take a look."

"You'll have to take that excursion on your own."

"I see how you are. Just for that I'm going to talk about how sucky the customer service is on my feedback card at checkout."

"Do it, and you'll never get extra towels ever again." She pouted, trying to hide her chuckle.

He laughed and stepped closer to the pool, turning when Kelsey tried to move past him. He snagged her around the waist and pulled her against him as they looked at the blue water glowing with underwater lights. She twisted in his arms, and Micah leaned down and kissed her, slow and sensual but hot like all kisses were when you first touched each other.

He tugged her closer until they were tight against each other, not even the slight breeze in the air was able to get between them. He was hard all over, the muscles under his skin flexing against her as she arched into him, desperate to get as much contact with him as she could.

"Who else lives here besides you and your friends?" he asked, his mouth trailing along the exposed skin of her shoulder. She shivered a little, either the chill in the night or his touch was raising goose bumps on her flesh.

"No one. The last unit is empty."

"Good." He grinned against her neck before pulling back to look down at her. "We can go for a swim without an audience."

She let him lead her around the edge of the pool to the shallow end where the lounge chairs were lined up like little soldiers.

"Did you wear a swimsuit under your jeans?" she asked, watching as he toed off his boots and kicked them to the side.

"Nope." Micah leaned down and pulled off his socks tossing them onto the pile with his boots. His grin took on that wicked edge that made her stomach clench when he flashed it her way. He reached over his head and gathered up the material of his T-shirt, pulling it up and over his head and dropping it to join his growing pile of clothing. His chest was a solid mass of muscle, his pecs covered with the right amount of dark hair that narrowed down his abs into the most lickable treasure trail. "Where I come from, we might not dance, but we do skinny-dip with a beautiful girl."

"Really?" Kelsey smiled, stepping lightly out of his reach when he reached out for her. Micah watched as she kicked off her shoes and dipped her toe in the water. It was warm after absorbing the heat of the day, and it would feel delicious against her skin. He would also feel delicious against her, but she wanted to draw out the anticipation just a little while longer. "We don't do a lot of skinny-dipping here in Vegas."

"Well that's a shame. You have the weather for it all year."

Damn. The slow drawl was back, covering the sex dripping from every word he said with slick, sweet honey that matched the moisture between her legs, making her wet. It was decision time. The precipice of taking this a step further and doing something with Micah she could never take back. But what scared her most was the whisper in her ear that there would be nothing with this man that she would want to take back. She felt the need to make sure they were on the same page.

"No strings," she said. He stopped all movement, his eyes sharp and focused on her. He looked solemn, as if he sensed how important this agreement between them was to her.

"No strings. No entanglements," he whispered, his voice a rough, silky glide of seduction carried across the short distance by the water and the hush of the secluded courtyard. "Kelsey, this is whatever you want it to be. I'm following your lead."

"That's what I want." It was also what she needed to keep whatever was happening between them separate and apart from her job.

Still, in the end there was no question that she was getting in the damn pool with him, but she still wanted to draw this moment out a little bit longer. Micah was watching her, his eyes tracking the swipe of her tongue along her lips, gaze dropping to see the heavy rise and fall of her chest as she tried to catch her breath. His hands dropped to the waistband of his jeans and she couldn't help but follow the movement, her body stepping forward to see him better in the scant light given off by the lights surrounding the pool.

"Take them off," she whispered, her voice husky and deep with her own need. She considered walking over and helping him with the task, but the sight of him unfastening the top button riveted her in place. Micah kept his eyes on her as he grasped the zipper pull and eased it down, shoving down his jeans and kicking them away in one, fluid motion.

"Now, you've got a choice here," Micah said, his voice low and gravely, making her shiver. He hooked two fingers in the waistband of his boxer briefs and tugged them down far enough for her to see the top of his dark pubic hair at the end of his happy trail. "I can leave these on, or I can take them off, too." He grinned, that lopsided twist of his mouth that made her want to bite his bottom lip. "Ladies' choice."

Kelsey took a step forward. Then another. And another. She was standing right in front of him and she reached out, her hands trembling from the want running through her veins. But her aim was sure, even though she never looked away from his face, and she added her own fingers to his where they rested against his waistband. The silence between them got hotter, thicker as it stretched out second by second until she thought she might break before it did.

"Take them off, too," she whispered and tugged down.

Micah sucked in a breath and then leaned forward, taking her mouth in a sweet, slow kiss. His eyes were still open, locked with hers, as they jointly eased his boxer briefs down.

She couldn't help it; Kelsey broke off the kiss and looked downward, the sight of his hard, thick cock compelling her to touch. One light stroke from root to tip and then a whisper-soft tracing of the vein that pulsed along the hard length of him.

"Fuck. Yeah." Micah groaned as he removed his underwear and kicked them to the side. He took one step and then two, shaking his head when she made a sound of protest at his abandonment of her. "If you want it, take off your clothes and join me in the pool."

And he turned and made a shallow dive into the water, his perfectly hard ass the last thing she saw before he plunged below the surface.

•••

The water did nothing to cool him off.

Not that it was that warm from the day's heat but the memory of Kelsey's brief touch of his dick made his skin burn all over. He surfaced, wiping the water off his face, and turned to see what she would do. Kelsey stood where he left her, the bluish glow from the pool lights illuminating her body with the silver reflection of the ripples. He took a step forward, the water just reaching the middle of his thighs where he stood in the shallows, the chill of the air reacting with his arousal to make him tense with heat and want and lust.

She was so goddamn gorgeous, and he couldn't take his eyes off her. She captivated him and had done so since the first time he'd seen her standing on his doorstep at the hotel, and now he was within seconds of being able to touch and kiss and have her sweet body wrapped around his cock. But first, she needed to get naked.

"Come on, Kelsey. You know you want to."

She stared him down for a moment, and he worried that

she wouldn't join him but then she kicked off one heel, and then the other. He smiled and she grinned back, just before she turned around and flashed him a sexy look over her shoulder.

Hell yeah, she wanted to play and he grabbed his dick, stroking it as he watched her. She crossed her arms, gathering the fabric of her tank top and pulled it over her head, giving him a full view of the sexy, satiny skin of her back. A hand reached around her back and he watched as she undid the clasp of her bra and let the slip of fabric fall to the ground.

"Turn around," he said, his voice harsher to his ears than he intended, but it produced the results he craved. Kelsey turned and faced him, her skin a dark caramel in the gloom of night, her brown nipples tight and hard where they stood out from the round, heavy globes of her breasts.

"Damn, baby. You're gorgeous," he said, more a moan than words, but she heard him and understood. Her chin jutted up with pride and not a little bit of defiance as if she needed to convince herself to continue. The thought that she might not join him hit him with a jolt of panic and he stroked himself, showing her how much the sight of her turned him on. "Come on, Kelsey. I need you."

That was all she needed because she shoved down her miniskirt and panties in one movement and let them drop to the ground. Her belly was flat, but curvy where it should be as it led to the dark patch of hair at the crux of her legs. Kelsey took two steps forward, following his path as she made a shallow dive into the pool and disappeared below the surface. He watched her progress under the ripples of water, waiting patiently until she turned and swam to him. She surfaced, her hand smoothing her hair from her face, the water sluicing down her body in rivulets that he envied for the way they got to caress her skin.

Micah reached out and grabbed her by the arms, pulling

her up against his body and took her lips in a kiss. Her lips were soft, cool, and yielding to the intrusion of his tongue inside her mouth. Inside she was delicious, sweet, and her tongue dueled with his as she sought his taste.

She trembled against him, and he dragged her closer resisting the urge to lift her up and ram up into her body and pound into her until she fell apart. But he could wait, draw it out, and make it good for both of them. He released her mouth and traced his lips along her cheek, sucking her earlobe between his teeth, taking a quick nip that made her moan and dig her nails into the flesh of his shoulders.

He lifted her up against his body and turned them until her back was against the side of the pool. Kelsey rubbed all over him, and he fucking loved it. It had been so long since he'd touched anyone that he was aching for the contact, not just his cock but his entire body. He lowered his head and indulged, licking and tasting every available square inch of her collarbone, the long, graceful column of her neck, and the sexy curves at the top of her breasts.

Micah loosened his grip a little and dipped down, licking at the hard nipple of one breast and then the other. Kelsey jerked against him, her legs opening wider and allowing him to press in close to the molten heat of her core. She ground herself against his erection, and they both cursed at the contact. He sucked harder on the taut peak, licking and laving at the gorgeous swell of her breast.

"I want to lick you all over. I bet you're sticky sweet like candy, and I won't stop until I taste all of you. Every inch," he murmured in the pause as he transferred his attention to her other breast.

"Yes. Please." Kelsey's fingers wove through his hair and kept him close as she offered her body to him. "More. Talk to me."

Fuck yeah, he could talk to her.

"I want to lick you here. Eat you up. I bet you're the sweetest in this very spot." He reached down and ran a finger across the lips of her sex. She was slick and wet already and not just from the water in the pool. He urged her up on the side of the pool, her legs spreading wider as he leisurely caressed her body, loving the moan that escaped past her lips as she arched against him. "I'll lick you here, make you wet, and then I'll eat that up too. Won't be able to get enough of it, I just know it."

Kelsey reached up and pulled him toward her, yanking him down until their lips met and she shut him up with her tongue in his mouth. It set him off like a bottle rocket, her need of him communicated through the rough possession of her kiss. He couldn't have stopped if his life depended on it, every piece of him primed to keep at it until she came all over him.

When they broke apart for air he let his head drop, his forehead against her shoulder as they gulped in oxygen. "I want to eat you up and then finger fuck you until you come, and when you're slick and ready and slippery enough to beg me to take you, I'll slide my cock in, slow and deep."

He grabbed her hand and lowered it to his dick, letting out a sigh of relief when her long fingers wrapped around him, and she stroked him with a firm but measured touch. Calculated to make him nuts but not to get him off. He bucked up into her grip, allowing himself the pleasure building inside him as she jacked him off, the roll of his hips encouraging her to continue.

"I want this," she said in between gulps of air. "I want you inside me, and I want everything you said. Please, Micah."

The sound of his name on her lips, the syllables wrapping around his shaft and his balls until he knew he was going to have to get her to stop or this was going to be over faster than his first time. He loved fooling around, the foreplay of the whole thing, but she needed to back off if any of that was going to happen.

"Open your legs wider," he said, lifting his head and pulling out of her grasp. Micah pressed kisses down her chest, laving each nipple with his tongue just to hear her gasp and to feel the dig of her nails in his bicep. Down her belly, across the sweet triangle of hair until he could see her, taste her.

He gripped her hips and urged her to tilt up to him, and he put his mouth on her and lapped at her pussy, moaning as her taste burst on his tongue. He suckled her, caressed her with hot, open-mouth kisses that had her groaning and twisting under him. It wouldn't take long, they were both so wound up. A couple of days of longing and verbal foreplay would do that.

Micah added a finger to his attention, pushing it inside her hot cleft and finding her hot and soft and ready for him. But he wanted her to come first because the first time would not be gentle; there was no way in hell he could guarantee that. He continued to kiss her folds, with slow, dragging licks of his tongue that spread around her delicious lube. He applied himself to his task, reveling in the way she moved underneath him, the grinding twist of her hips against his mouth as she sought to take what she wanted, no longer patient to wait.

"Yeah, Kelsey. Take what you need. Use me to feel good," he murmured against her skin and then transferred his focus to her clit.

She thrashed a little underneath him, her hands in his hair, tugging and pulling him even closer to the *V* between her thighs and then she went bowstring taut. Her entire body was arching up toward the moonlight, and he angled his head to see it all: the elegant bend of her body, the sharp, tight peaks of her breasts thrusting upward.

"Oh. My. Fucking. God." Her cry was deep, guttural as she came, loud in the hush of the secluded courtyard.

He kissed his way up her body, lingering in the dips and hollows, licking the soft curves until he could cover her mouth with his. She opened to him, her hands touching everywhere she could reach as if the orgasm had only sparked her appetite and not satisfied her hunger. Good. He wanted her as desperate for him as he was for her.

She trailed her fingers down his chest, lingering over his nipples with feather-light swirls that made him gasp, and then lower until her fingers closed around him again. Micah pulled back enough to look at her, their mouths still glancing against each other as he almost lost himself in the wicked, hot depths of her eyes.

"That was…" she whispered, her voice shaky and uneven. She licked her lips as her hand began a slow stroke that he pumped into. "I want more."

"Greedy girl." He chuckled, breaking off when her thumb swiped the sensitive head of his cock. "I'll give you more. Anything you want as long as it is done with me inside you, deep and hard."

"Yes." She nodded, releasing her hold on him as he leaned over to snag his jeans and pull them over.

He fished the couple of condoms out of his pocket and then lifted her slightly to place the denim under her back and hips.

"Here?" she asked, her eyes on him as he opened the packet and rolled the condom down his shaft.

"Yeah. Fucking here. You okay with that?" Micah looked up at her, his hand idly gripping his length and stepped in closer until he could rub the tip of his penis up and down the wet length of her sex. She moaned and pushed back in a rhythm that was only calculated to get him to stop teasing her and get inside her.

He could definitely oblige.

Micah pushed inside her, the heat of her tight body

searing him through the latex and pulling him like a man starved after too many days in the desert. Her body was lush, giving, slick and tight, and he could not resist. She spread her legs further, lifting her hips up to meet his thrust and he slid home in one long push.

"Goddamn, Kelsey. You feel like a dream."

"You're awake," she said, her hands skimming over the skin of his chest, down his arms, and up to tangle in his wet hair. He leaned into her touch, soaking up every sensation as he immersed all of his senses into this moment with her.

Micah slid out of her body until only the tip of him remained inside her. They stared at each other, his body shaking with the effort to make this connection last before he lost what little control he had left.

She grabbed his hips, her fingers digging into his skin, emphasizing her urgent plea. "Please, Micah. Move. Fill me up. Please."

It was the permission he needed to give in to his own raging lust, and he surged forward, pulling out and gritting his teeth at the clinging caress of her channel. He leaned over her, hands braced on the concrete on each side of her head, the position keeping them eye-to-eye as he covered her with his body and thrust deep. She jerked out a shuddery sob each time he snapped his hips and sank into her heat.

The combination of her desperate sounds and the way her body opened to him was enough to get him to the edge and keep him there, hovering so close to coming that his vision went dark on the edges. It was her second orgasm that tipped him over. He watched, mesmerized by her soundless abandonment to her pleasure, the jerk of her hips against his own as she squeezed her breasts and nipples and came all over his cock.

"Fuck, you're gorgeous. Fuck." He leaned down and took her mouth, half panting and half moaning as he drove in deep and spent himself in a long, toe-curling orgasm. He fucked into her body, continuing the hard thrust as he rode it out, extending it for as long as he could because the thought of having to leave her slick, hot, wet, yielding body made him ache. "Take me. Take it."

"Yes. Yes." Kelsey chanted in a loop of half words and raged breaths as she collapsed against the pool deck in a boneless heap.

Micah lowered himself, maintaining as much full-body contact as he could while he greedily explored her mouth. He did not want this to end, the aftershocks of pleasure causing his cock to pulse inside her in a valiant effort to make a repeat performance. Kelsey kissed him back, her hands looping around his neck, fingers lightly tracing the slope of his shoulders as they came down from the contact high of skin-on-skin.

"Are you okay?" he asked, lifting his head to look into her eyes. She was slow to meet his gaze, her eyes unfocused when she finally did meet his own. "You good?"

"Don't sell yourself short. That was perfect," she said. She stretched out, her arms extending out as he slipped from her body. Micah admired the long, toned line of her body, and he suddenly didn't want the night to end. "We need to do that in a bed next time. I want to ride you, but not on this concrete."

Micah chuckled, reaching out his hand to help her up. "Is that an invitation to stay?"

He had no idea if their arrangement allowed for sleepovers, but he hoped it did.

"This might be temporary, but I'm a better hostess than to come and then kick you out." She walked over to her pile of clothes and bent over to pick them up. The position gave him an excellent view of her tight ass, and he knew that the next round would involve him driving into her from behind with that view on display. His cock started to harden, wholeheartedly agreeing to his plan.

Micah covered the distance, intending to tell her exactly what he planned when three loud, drunken voices popped up at the security gate to the courtyard. The low rumble of Aiden's voice told him her friends had departed the club earlier than expected. Kelsey's head whipped up, her eyes wide with shock and alarm.

"Oh crap." She scooped her clothes up and gestured toward a doorway to the left of the pool. She dropped her bra and had to scrabble for it again as a laugh burst from her mouth. "Move it, or my friends are going to get an up-close-and-personal view of your junk."

"What? Are you afraid that if they get a look at my personal assets you might have a fight on your hands?" He grabbed his own pile of clothes, having to snag his Converse twice before he got a solid grip on them and followed her in a mad dash for the shadows near her door and the safety inside her place.

Kelsey fumbled with her keys, looking over her shoulder as the shouts and laughter of her best friends got closer and closer. She flashed a glance at him, her grin wide, cheeky, and oh so naughty. He loved it.

"And for the record, there would be no fights. I don't share. No matter how temporary the arrangement is."

He blinked, his dick getting harder at the sound of possession in her voice. He could handle the lust but it was the surge of ownership in his own gut when he thought of her with another guy. Micah pushed it down and cleared his voice before answering her.

"No sharing. I'm on board with that."

"Good." She pushed the door open and crooked a finger for him to follow. "Drop your clothes on the floor. You won't be needing them anymore tonight."

Chapter Eleven

It was way too early to be up.

The smell of brewing coffee teased Kelsey as she rolled over in her bed, burying her head under her pillow with a groan. But she was up now, the lure of liquid caffeine drawing her out of her sleepy haze. She reached out and snagged her phone from the nightstand and looked at the screen, wincing at the crazy time of the morning. They'd gone to sleep a couple of hours earlier, exhausted after three rounds of the best sex of her life.

She stretched, tossing her phone back toward the general direction of the side table, not caring when it missed and made a loud *thunk* on the floor. In spite of the early hour, she felt too good to care. Her body ached in that way that gives you a secret smile all day when you remember every kiss and thrust and clench from a night of being well used. She let the memories of the night before roll through her mind as the tingles and shivers passed over her skin, and she smiled the smug smile of the thoroughly fucked.

It was times like this that she wondered why she waited

so long between bed partners.

The sound of ceramic mugs being placed on the tiled surface in her kitchen was the motivation she needed to go seek out her current bedmate, that and the potent brew that would be the only thing to get her through the day on so little sleep. Kelsey reached out and snagged her short, kimono-styled silk robe off the bench at the foot of the bed and slipped it on. She made her way down the short hallway to the kitchen, surprised when she didn't find Micah in that end of the room.

Her place wasn't huge, so it took only a quick scan to locate him, bent over at the waist, tight ass showcased in his jeans and his cut back muscles left exposed as he peered down at the photos lined up on her bookcases. She watched him for a few moments, noticing his intense interest, the way he reached out and touched certain photographs with soft, lingering swipes of his finger. Her gut twisted a little with the knowledge that he was seeing her life…her real life…and she knew questions would follow. Questions she wasn't used to answering from the guys she slept with.

That's what she got for bringing him home with her. It wasn't that she hadn't calculated it in her tally of just how bad an idea this really was. Her final calculation had placed it somewhere between the zombie apocalypse and her unfortunate attempt at pixie haircut in the ninth grade, but it hadn't stopped her. Getting involved with a tourist. Getting involved with a guest at the hotel. She'd known that unless she booted him out the door in the wee hours of the morning, he would get a peek behind the curtain. Taking him to some random hotel hadn't appealed at all, and that feeling had overridden her desire to keep him at an arm's length.

She ducked behind the breakfast bar not even trying to be quiet as she picked up the mug Micah had placed on the counter and poured a cup of the hot stuff. When she turned, he was standing in the same place, a soft smile on his lips as he stared at her. He was hot with his dark hair rumpled and his eyes warm but also heavy with his own lack of sleep.

"Good morning," he said, tracking her with his eyes as she made her way across the room to stand next to him.

"It is morning but it's too early to be good," she said, hoping the smile she could feel tugging at her mouth would take away any of the sting from her words.

It didn't appear to deter Micah as he leaned in and pressed his lips against hers in a kiss as sweet as the sugar she never took in her coffee. His flesh was warm and soft against her own, and she didn't even notice that she was leaning into him, following the lead of his hand which was suddenly cupping the back of her neck. Fuck, but he killed her with his kisses. He was world-class, stellar, toe-curlingly good.

Every kiss flared the passion between them again as it had after round two early this morning. In the only attempt for him to leave, Micah had kissed her, intending it to be good-bye, and it had left them sweaty and wrapped up in each other on the rug in her bedroom.

"Does that improve your assessment of the morning being 'good'?" Micah asked, his breath warm on her cheek as he skimmed along her skin, stopping only to deliver a tender bite against the skin of her neck.

Kelsey shivered, laughing softly as he leaned his forehead on her shoulder and the seconds passed by them in a comfortable way she didn't have with many people. Micah was a surprise, one that pleased and puzzled her, as she tried to keep their relationship in the right box. The sex part was easy but the compatibility, the easy way between them was harder to pigeonhole.

Micah lifted his head, turning back to the bookcase while taking a sip of his coffee. He gestured toward a photo of her parents taken about five years ago on the back patio of the house. Her mom was in her father's lap as usual, since they couldn't be in the same space without touching each other.

"Are these your folks?" He glanced back at her. "You look like your mom."

Kelsey hesitated to answer, her first inclination to suggest that she call him a cab to go back to the hotel, and it must have been written all over her face because he quickly backtracked.

"Did I ask the wrong thing?" He stepped away, running his free hand through his hair with more embarrassment than irritation. "I'm not sure where the boundaries are here, Kelsey."

Defensiveness rose up in her chest, and her words flew out of her mouth much harsher than she intended. "The boundaries are easy. This is temporary. We have sex. You leave. I stay."

"So, is asking questions about family off-limits? I can go down on you for hours, but I can't ask about a photo in your living room?" He stared her down and she shuffled a little on her bare feet with the intensity of his stare. "I know this is what it is, but we've been friendly enough so far without causing any type of international incident. If I wanted a girl to let me fuck her, I could have rented one of those by the hour."

When he put it that way, it sounded ridiculous. It wasn't like they hadn't talked before about things in their lives, she'd taken him to meet her friends. She liked Micah. It didn't have to change the rules to tell him about a damn photo.

"You're right." She offered up a smile and reached for the photo, handing it over to him. "I'm just…twitchy."

"Twitchy," he said, his expression and his tone flat with a hint of confused.

"Yeah, twitchy. You make me twitchy."

"I'm presuming that isn't as bad as it sounds since you let me make you feel other things at least five times last night." His smirk was back, and Kelsey wondered again how he could be so laid-back and easy to talk to.

"You make all of this too easy," she said, waiting to see if he understood what she was really saying. Micah stared at her for a couple of beats, his eyes assessing her and then warming with his understanding and agreement. "*That* makes me twitchy."

He broke eye contact first, and she felt the loss of the warmth in his deep brown eyes, but she also felt relief. Shit was getting way too serious in here.

"Yeah, I know what you mean. The rules don't cover everything going on here between us," he murmured while still gazing down at the photograph. She struggled with how to answer that, but he wasn't expecting one and didn't leave her any space to fill. "They are a beautiful couple together."

She looked at the photo, one of her favorites, and she knew what he saw. Her father was a large man with gorgeous dark skin and his hair cut very short, smile wide and open. Her mother was tall as well, her skin a stunning mocha shade that was beautifully matched by her coppery, butterscotch eyes, her dark hair long and curly. Kelsey was a perfect mix of her parents with her skin a deep caramel, her father's copper brown eyes, and her mom's dimpled grin.

"They were so much in love, best friends, but they could fight over politics like the world was on fire. They took great pride in canceling out each other's votes, but they both adored Japanese food and agreed on how to put the toilet paper on the bar thingy."

"You put it on there so that the TP rolls down from the top."

She grinned at him, patting him on the head like an obedient pet. "Exactly."

Micah shook off her touch with a grin and a roll of his eyes. "Your parents sound like mine. They make you believe that all that stuff I write about is possible."

"My folks had it. I'd bet all the money in Vegas on that fact."

She knew that her tone gave away her own wistfulness over ever having that kind of love in her own life. She didn't really care right now. She wanted it. Who wouldn't?

"I'm sorry, I didn't know your mother had passed," he said, watching her intently. "I hope I didn't bring up a tough subject for you to talk about."

Kelsey squirmed, realizing too late that she'd caused his misunderstanding and walked right into a part of her life that was difficult to share with her best friends, much less an almost stranger. But none of her warning bells had gone off when they'd moved to the topic of family with Micah.

"She's still alive," she said and for a split second she thought about covering it up and telling him she'd misspoken, but she didn't want to do that. She wanted to tell him about this part of her life. As usual, talking with him was like talking with someone she'd known forever. This guy was different, and she was glad he was leaving on Sunday or she could be in big trouble. "She's suffering from early onset dementia and has been in a nursing care facility for eighteen months. It's a toss-up on any given day if she even knows who I am. She remembers my dad more often."

"Oh," Micah said, his gaze fixed on her own as he obviously struggled to figure out what to say. She opened her mouth to spare him the effort but he beat her to it, and what he said had her stepping closer and letting him put his arms around her and drag her to him in a loose but warm embrace. "That's got to be even harder on you, to see her still here but know that inside she's lost."

How did he know? How did he have any idea what kept her up nights and had her weeping in the hallway outside her mom's room so her dad didn't see?

"My dad has it worse. He misses his best friend," she

murmured, her face buried in the dip of his shoulder, his warm skin and scent washing over her in silent comfort. "But he says that we at least have the memories she's lost. We have that comfort, and she...doesn't. We loved each other, laughed a lot, and supported each other."

"It sounds like you had a happy childhood," Micah said, his voice low and soothing as it vibrated against her cheek. She looked at him, wondering how he made that accurate leap from all the heavy stuff she said. He must have read her thoughts because he chuckled and took the photo from her, running his thumb across the glass. "I'm not one of those guys on the Strip who reads mind. It wasn't much of a leap to know that a kid who grows up knowing her parents love each other that much is likely to have a happy childhood."

"You speak like you know from experience."

"I do. My folks sound like your parents. I always had the security of knowing they adored each other. That makes a kid secure and happy. It set the bar pretty high for my own marriage."

She remembered that he was divorced, but he'd never spoken about it in the press, so she wasn't sure how big a failure his marriage really was. All she could do was ask, and if he told her that it was none of her business, fair enough. This thing between them was in a weird space, and they were negotiating its terms minute-by-minute it seemed.

"And your marriage? How far off the mark was it?"

...

Micah released his hold on Kelsey and placed her photograph back on the shelf, turning his body so she couldn't see his face clearly. It was a move calculated to give him some privacy from her prying question, even though he knew he was going to answer. It hadn't been easy for Kelsey to share that fact about her mom, and the least he could do was return the show of trust.

"Well, since I count being faithful as one of those basic things to make a marriage successful, I'd say we missed the mark pretty spectacularly," he said on a sigh that rumbled down deep in his gut. When would the knowledge of what happened stop making him feel like shit?

"She had to be crazy. Who would cheat on you?" Kelsey clapped her mouth shut pretty quickly, her expression telling him that she blurted it out before she could stop herself. It gave away more of her feelings about him than she really wanted to reveal, but that was okay by him. He liked Kelsey, and he was glad to know she liked him, too, even if they couldn't keep each other.

He laughed a little before he launched into his answer, the taste of it both bitter and sweet on his tongue.

"We were sweethearts from elementary school, married right after high school, and then I went to boot camp. I don't think either of us was prepared for life in the military much less being married. We had never lived anywhere but Bridger Gap, and suddenly she was left alone on a military base with nobody while I was halfway across the world."

He was trying to a gentleman, to be fair. Yes, Becky was the one who broke the vow, but he hadn't been that great a husband, putting the Corps before her in everything and not really sympathizing when she'd told him how lonely she was and asked to go back home while he was deployed. Looking back on that time, it felt like two kids playing at being grown-ups.

Kelsey wasn't so understanding, and she didn't hide her irritation on his behalf. "It's not like it was a huge surprise either. Everyone knows what being a member of the military means these days. It's no picnic for anybody."

"I'm not making excuses for her. Becky cheated on me

with a guy I'd been friends with since we were in diapers, and that shit hurt," he said, his tone carrying more of an edge than it should after all this time. "I woke up in the hospital in Germany with a head injury from the IED and my parents were there with the news that my wife wasn't going to be waiting for me when I got home."

"She didn't even tell you herself?" Now Kelsey was pissed and he couldn't help but admire the way her cheeks flushed pink when she was angry. It was cute and sexy and made him want to pick her up and carry her back to bed. "There is being young and there is being a cowardly bitch, and I know where I put the former Mrs. Holmes right now."

Her reaction made him smile; he didn't necessarily disagree with her assessment of his ex-wife, but Kelsey's outrage was so genuine, so visceral that it made him happy down in the very sick part of his brain that wanted her to give a shit about him. He reached out and grabbed one of her hands, feeling the jump of her pulse point on her wrist as he slid their fingers together. After what they'd done last night, holding hands was pretty tame, but it shot warmth over his skin that he allowed himself to revel in, soaking in her vitality.

"She wrote me a letter, but it came after I was injured. My parents knew and when they came to the hospital in Germany, they got the honor of breaking the news." She squeezed his hand, adjusting their grip so that her hand covered his own. It was an intimate gesture, one that touched him more than the sex they'd had last night. It reached below the surface and beyond the nerve endings and latched onto that vulnerable spot located just behind his ribs. "Your face looks just like my mom's did when she told me what had happened with Becky."

"Well, I hope so," she said, her words dripping with her heated irritation. "That was a pretty shitty thing to do."

"Yeah, but looking back on all of it, it was probably never going to work. We loved each other, but it wasn't the kind that could stand up to what life threw at us and that was the truth. My deployment just made us realize it sooner rather than later."

"I don't know how you write the books you write if that is what happened to you," Kelsey said.

"I guess I'm writing about how I would like for it to have been." He shrugged and drew her to him, his nose brushing along her jaw as he pressed a soft kiss here and there. She leaned into it and he realized that he hadn't kissed her this morning. Not properly. He fixed that ridiculous oversight, pressing his mouth softly to hers, the tangle of their tongues remaining sweet and easy. He pulled back, looking down at her as her eyes opened slowly on a sexy, dazed blink of her long, dark lashes. Micah somehow continued what he was saying. "Or the way I think it should be, and hope I might have one day."

"Do you really think that's possible?" she asked, her voice a smoky whisper.

"I've seen it, and so have you. It's like the lottery, right? Somebody is going to win it, and it might as well be me."

"They also say that you have to play to win," she said. Her smile was twisted, an attempt at sarcasm but he saw the wistful expression in her eyes.

"I didn't think you were inclined to play that game," he said, keeping his voice neutral with the hope that he'd get some insight into this intriguing woman.

"I hit my three strikes, and I took myself out."

"Permanently?"

"I've never met anyone who made me change my decision."

"So the right guy…"

"The right guy could change lots of things." Kelsey stared at him when she said it and he thought he sensed a dare in her eyes to change her mind, and he almost took the conversation further but she blinked and dropped his hand, turning back toward the kitchen. "I'm warming up my coffee."

Micah almost followed her, but what was the point? He wasn't staying past Sunday and she wasn't asking. Instead, he placed his coffee cup down on a side table, turned and continued his review of her shelves, interested in what kind of book Kelsey would choose. The entire wall of her living room was covered in floor-to-ceiling shelves with books stacked two deep on many of them. College textbooks, travel guides, and various "for Dummies" volumes took up a little bit of space and then they gave way to fiction.

Thrillers and suspense, popular mainstream novels, and a couple Tom Clancy books and then it became romance. Every kind of romance: historical, paranormal, contemporary, young adult. Every big name and some he didn't recognize, new and old. He lifted a Bertrice Small and thumbed over to the copyright page, noting that it was likely from a first or second mass market paperback printing, and it had been well-read and loved. Coffee stains, scratches, and creases covered the front and the pages within.

He'd arrived at the shelf with his books lined up in a row, and she reached around him and pointed to *Safe Harbor*.

"That's my favorite one of yours," she said, her body brushing against his.

"Why?" It was probably vain to ask, but he was curious.

"Two words: hammock sex." Kelsey waggled her eyebrows and he laughed, sliding an arm around her waist and pulled her back until her back touched his entire front. He placed a kiss on the skin exposed by the slide of her T-shirt off her shoulder, loving the way her giggle vibrated against his lips.

"Lots of readers love that scene," he answered.

"Because it was freaking hot."

"Thanks." Micah leaned in even closer, letting his eyes wander over the line up of books he really didn't want to write. The question now was whether he had the balls to quit or not.

"Are you really going to stop writing romance? Do you really hate them so much?" she asked, and he bit back a laugh of surprise that she seemed to know his own train of thought.

"I don't think I hate writing them."

He turned over his feelings and tried to examine every inch before he answered. "I think I hate feeling like I don't have the option to write anything else."

"You could self-publish, some of my favorite authors do that. Then you could write whatever you want for yourself and then the romance for your fans."

"You sound like Allen."

"Well, obviously he's brilliant." She laughed.

"Jesus, don't ever tell him that."

"So if you know you can do whatever you want, then what's stopping you? Why keep letting the people at the publisher tell you no?" Kelsey asked, turning in his arms to look him right in the eye. "You've got a name and connections, and I hope you've made some money from the books and the movies."

Micah fought the urge to squirm but he did break eye contact, leaning his head back to puff out a long sigh at how her words cut him to the quick. She was honest, and he found himself unable to do anything but reciprocate.

"I don't know...ego...hurt pride at having them turn down my ideas...the sheer amount of fucking incredible work that would have to go into self-publishing."

"So..." She dragged her words out and didn't mince any of the sarcasm that dripped from every syllable. "You're holding yourself hostage because you're ass hurt that they don't want to play in your sandbox, and you're afraid of hard work?" She shook her head and gave him a look that told him exactly what she thought of his reasoning. "Nope. I don't buy it. I've only known you for a short time, and that guy is not you."

"He's not?"

"No. And you want to know how I know?" Kelsey asked as she leaned in so close that their mouths almost touched. Micah swallowed, tightening his grip on her hips as he involuntarily drew her warm, sexy body to his. She didn't wait for him to respond to her question. "Because that guy would never have convinced me to invite him into my bed last night."

Micah stared down at her, exploring every inch of her expression and was floored by the conviction of her words in the depths of her eyes and the set of her jaw. She was right. Somewhere in the last few years, he'd become the guy who took no for an answer and went along with the tide. The same guy who'd let his failed marriage, and the women who only wanted to use him, keep him holed up in his cabin in Bridger Gap and away from real life. But down deep he was there, the old Micah. The one who took chances and risked even his own life to do what he knew was right. It was that Micah that had kept pushing Kelsey to let him in, and he could still taste on his lips just how right that risk had been to take.

He lowered his head and took her mouth, letting the adrenaline rush caused by her words, and his reaction, fuel his desire for her. Kelsey responded, looping her arms around his neck and wrapped her legs around his waist when he slid his hands under her ass and lifted her to him. The bookcases behind them shook a little with the momentum of their bodies.

Her quick exhale on impact broke the kiss and dissolved into a low chuckle as their eyes met. Their laughter didn't stop the next press of mouths and sweep of tongue, adding fuel to the fire between them instead of dampening it. Micah resolved to turn and lay her down on the couch behind them when a loud beeping from down the hall rang out into the stillness of the morning.

It was an alarm clock. Kelsey's alarm clock.

"No. No. No," she mumbled against his lips, as the sound got louder and more frequent as they continued to kiss, pulling back only to dive back in as soon as breathing and logistics would allow. But the machine would not be ignored and finally forced them apart, and she pulled away and sprinted down the hallway toward her room. He caught a glimpse of her bare ass cheek when her movement lifted the edge of her robe, and he was tempted to follow her and strip it off her, but a glance at the clock told him that their time was up for now.

Two loud slaps of flesh against something, and a muffled curse from her, and the screeching stopped, the silence ringing with the lingering vibrations.

"That was the most obnoxious sound I have ever heard. Is it broken, or is it supposed to sound like that?" he asked, watching as she reappeared in the living room.

"I bought it because it's guaranteed to never let you oversleep. I've been known to hit the snooze and wake up three days later."

"You'd have to be deaf to sleep through that noise." Micah moved around the sofa and reached out, snagging the belt on her robe and dragged her to him. She gave a token struggle but melted into his arms as he pulled her back into a kiss that lingered. He pulled back enough to murmur against her mouth. "You've got to go to work?"

She nodded, releasing a little sigh as she leaned her forehead against his. "Yeah. I've got this high maintenance guest I have to look after *all day*."

"He sounds like a dick," he said, tracing his hand along the sleek skin of her thigh and under the edge of her robe, cupping the sweet curve of her ass in his palm. Her skin broke out in goose bumps under his touch. "Let me make it up to you tonight?"

She cocked her head, the smile lifting her mouth in a wicked twist that made his gut clench with excitement. "Don't you have a book to finish today?"

He nodded, anxious to see where she was going with this. "Yes."

"If you finish the book, I'll make it up to *you*."

"Consider it done."

Chapter Twelve

Running usually cleared his mind. Usually.

But not this morning. After six miles through the streets of Las Vegas, Micah could not get Kelsey Kyle out of his head, and he really needed to get her out. First, he had a book to write, and she took up too much headspace in there. Secondly, he was leaving on Sunday. This was temporary and he could not afford to get emotionally invested in her, no matter how much his long-dormant heart was screaming for him to do it. All these years of bad dates, disastrous relationships with women who "should" have worked for him, and the traitorous organ under his ribs decides to perk up and beat faster whenever Kelsey Kyle smiled at him.

And after last night, his heart wasn't the only thing that sat up and took notice when she was around. He'd wanted her before, but a night spent between her thighs morphed his casual hormonal reaction to her into something resembling the horny teenager he'd been long before heartache and a tour in hell had made him a man who did everything in a way calculated to minimize any exposure to potential hurt. It also accomplished the opposite and kept him from experiencing anything close to the highs of life, things like skinny-dipping with a girl whose kisses short-circuited his brain.

Micah removed his earbud, and the quiet after such an extended period of time with Metallica blaring in his ears was enough to cause him to stumble, his equilibrium temporarily compromised. The cool of the AC in the deserted lobby pebbled his skin with goose bumps, and he suppressed a shiver as he stopped in front of the elevator doors and swiped the pad with his room key.

Thoughts of completing his book and the reward of another night spent inside Kelsey meant he was surprised when a warm hand stoked over his shoulder and down his bicep. Micah jumped, pitching himself back toward the doors just as they opened, and he barely corrected in time to avoid falling face first into the car. A high-pitched giggle and a lower throaty chuckle joined his grunt of surprise as he righted himself and turned to see who it was.

He recognized the woman: tall and blonde and dripping in jewelry and beauty products from the top of her gravity-defying hair to her stiletto-wearing feet. She was definition of "trophy wife" and one glance at her older, less-attractive spouse convinced him that she worked hard for every penny.

Micah didn't like that she'd put her hands on him, but his memory reminded him that she was a fan and a VIP client for Kelsey. The longer he stared, he recalled her presence at his signing the day before and the way her hands had wandered over him just as freely. Whoever she was, she had issues with the concept of personal space.

"Did I surprise you?" she asked, as if she hadn't just watched him almost face-plant on the marble floor.

His manners kicked in and prevented him from saying what sprung to the tip of his tongue. Instead he went for the innocuous. "I don't usually see anyone else up this early."

"Can you be up this early when you haven't gone to bed?" she asked, her sentence ending on a purr as she advanced on him across the elevator.

Micah backed up as far as he could and cursed the chill of the mirrored wall when it hit his back. He was trapped in here with Mrs. Grabby Hands and her hubby who resembled one of the guys from *The Godfather* when they'd had a bad day.

"Wow. You must be beat then," he stammered, praying that no one else was awake to stop the upward progress of the elevator. "You'll be ready to hit the sack, I bet."

Blondie cut a sly glance at her husband and instead of the glower he expected, the man smiled. Everything in his body yelled "oh shit" as she turned back to him. Whatever she was going to say was something he didn't want to hear.

"I'm not tired," she said, brushing her breasts against the bare skin of his arm. He could either scurry back like a spooked reptile, or stand his ground. He opted to use the balls that were currently not responding to all the pheromones Blondie was throwing in his direction. "I've still got lots of energy to burn off." Another sloe-eyed glance at her husband and she pushed her body fully into him and started to let her hand wander down his abdomen before giving him her full attention. "You could join me." Another look at her hubby and back at him. "He likes to watch."

He wasn't new to getting hit on. Women frequently propositioned him, but this chick was a pro that made all the others look like poor auditions for the understudy. Micah stared at her, his gaze traveling to her husband, who confirmed her statement with a nod. Oh, fuck no. Even if he had been inclined, this had all the earmarks of a bad scene just waiting to happen, with the end result being his body in a shallow grave in the desert. He'd seen *Goodfellas*. It could happen.

She might be using sex as her tool, but she was no different than the women who'd been tailing him since he'd hit the NYT list. He didn't fool himself for one minute that she really wanted him. No, she wanted Micah Holmes, semi-famous author, in between her thighs so she could check him off some list or brag to her friends at the weekly trophy wife meeting.

"Oh. That's…" He had a million words in his head and spun them on the page every day, but not one of them came to mind. Micah opened his mouth and prayed it was the right thing. "That's really nice, but I'm going to have to pass. Really…no thank you, Mrs…"

"Forasch. Babette Forasch."

"We met yesterday, forgive me for not remembering." The cab stopped and time slowed down to a crawl as he waited for the doors to slide open and give him an escape route. The universe finally took pity on him and they slid back, and he edged around her to step onto his floor, dismayed when they disembarked with him. Mr. Forasch played with his room keycard, and Micah groaned inwardly with the knowledge that these people were on his floor.

Great.

He propelled himself down the hallway, hoping that the God he prayed to wasn't preoccupied with all of the pleas for help wafting up from the casino floor. He wanted to get to his door, open it, and escape from the potential for a threesome that would likely turn him off sex for the rest of his life. Now that he had Kelsey in his bed—or he was in hers—he wasn't going to jeopardize it.

He reached his door and swiped the keycard, the color green on the metal box now his official favorite color. The Forasches were right behind him lingering in the hallway, and he felt compelled by his goddamn southern manners to turn and say good-bye.

"Have good day," he said.

"We're in Room 4045 if you change your mind," Babette

said with a giggle and a shimmy of her very large breasts.

Micah had nothing, so he merely stepped across the threshold of his room and shut the door, heading for the hottest shower he could stand before he got to work.

...

Kelsey looked down at her watch and wondered where the morning had gone.

The convention was now fully underway with hordes of readers all over the hotel and workshops, panels, and signings in every available space. She had to admit to a couple of fangirl moments when two of her favorite authors were nearby, but she kept it completely professional since she didn't have time to ask for autographs.

Besides, her favorite author was holed up in his room finishing his book and also hiding from the crowds. They'd agreed on a time when she could come and pry him out of the suite and take him to his first panel of the day. It would be a long day for Micah, ending with the "Bring Your Hero to Dinner" event where he would have a meal and dance with some of his biggest fans. He was probably trying to figure out a way to sneak out of the hotel right now.

Her earpiece buzzed, and she tapped the device answering the call, "Kyle."

It was Perry.

"Kelsey, did you hear about the incident last night?"

She paused, wondering when Perry had decided to join in with the staff gossip. Everyone was talking about the shit that had gone down in the hotel last night.

"I did, and I'm wondering when that became legal in the state of Nevada."

"Our lawyers are working on that question, but that's not why I called." He cleared his throat. "Kelsey, I need you to come to the concierge lounge immediately."

Oh hell. He sounded grumpier than his usual self, and didn't that just jump up and bite her in the ass?

"On my way." She disconnected the call and made her way through the crowd to the office, wondering what else Perry was going to put on her plate for today. She was chock-full, but that had never stopped him before.

A few short moments later she pushed open the glass outer doors to the concierge lounge and left the loud roar of the convention behind her. The change was a little unsettling, and it took her a few moments to reorient herself to the peace of the office space. She heard voices from the direction of Perry's office and headed straight there, only slowing her steps down when she recognized who was in the room with him.

Saul and Babette Forasch. Shit. This wasn't going to end well. If she were a betting gal, she'd put it all on the line.

Perry looked up as she entered the room, and his smile was grim and laced with an edge of "how could you leave me with these people?" She got it. She really did.

"Mr. and Mrs. Forasch," she said, hoping her enthusiasm would make up for the fact that she didn't have the answer they wanted. "Are you enjoying your stay?"

"I'd enjoy it more if I had my VIP time with Micah Holmes," Babette said on a babyish pout that didn't quite disguise the warning in her eyes. Kelsey's skin tingled with the awareness that this woman might look like a young, clueless trophy wife, but it was a facade put in place to hide the conniving, ambitious woman underneath. Saul better have an ironclad prenup, or this one was going to leave him with nothing.

"Mrs. Forasch, I think I explained to you at the beginning that Mr. Holmes is extremely reluctant to do those types of events."

"And you assured me you could make it happen." She

turned her gaze to Perry and pointed with one long, fake fingernail. "You told me she could do this."

Perry flashed her a glance that told her she needed to fix this immediately. The Masquerade did not like to disappoint its highest of high rollers.

"I'm not saying no, but I am saying that I need more time." That was the understatement of the century, but she still believed she could figure out a way to make this palatable to Micah. Desperate times called for desperate measures. She'd watched him with his fans and knew how to put him at ease, so there had to be a way to get Babette the one-on-one time she wanted, but still keep Micah comfortable. *There had to be a way*. She could figure this out, she always did. "I'll be working with him again today, and I'll try to find a time to approach him with the suggestion."

"Don't *suggest*," Saul barked out, his arm slipping around Babette's waist. "Make it happen."

"You two looked pretty cozy yesterday at the signing," Babette said with more than a little whine in her tone. "Really cozy."

Kelsey froze in place, refusing to swing her gaze toward Perry even though she could feel his eyes on her. Babette knew nothing. She didn't know anything about last night. She was just observing how well she and Micah worked together, and there was no reason to panic that her secret was out.

"We worked together well yesterday. It's my job to make all the guests comfortable and to assist however I am needed. Mr. Holmes is easy to work with, and we performed well as a team yesterday."

She stopped talking knowing that anything else she said might give her away. Keep it professional. Keep it on task. Her phone buzzed with a text message, and she excused herself to check it. The name "M. Holmes" ran across the top, and she tapped the screen to read the message. It was one line. Three letters: SOS

Kelsey glanced at the clock on the phone and realized his first panel of the day was less than an hour away, and a distress signal at this time was not going to be a good thing.

"Pardon me. I have an emergency…with the convention." She made eye contact with the Forasches, hoping they didn't drag this out any longer. "I will let you know my progress soon."

Kelsey turned and beat feet out of there before they could stop her, her mind wondering what was up with Micah. He was supposed to be writing so what kind of emergency could he have?

Laptop charger not working?

Food?

More of those damn extra towels?

She moved across the lobby, nodding to the other staff and smiling at the guests as she stepped onto the elevator and slid her passcard through the reader to allow her to get to the executive level. She pressed the button for the fortieth floor and then tapped her Bluetooth earpiece and commanded the phone to dial Micah. He answered after one and a half rings.

"Kelsey, get up here now. This is serious."

"Are you okay?" The doors opened and she stepped out onto the carpeted hallway, picking up her pace with no guests in the corridor to see her. "I'm almost there."

A few short steps and she knocked on his door, surprised when it flew open immediately, and Micah reached out with the hand that wasn't holding his phone to tug her inside and shut the door behind her. Kelsey let her gaze roam all over him, trying to spot whatever it was that was causing the crisis. Micah lowered his phone from his ear and thumbed off the call, one eyebrow raised to match the smirk tugging at his lips.

"There's no emergency, is there?"

He smiled.

Chapter Thirteen

"You're such a dick!" Kelsey said.

She smacked Micah, the warmth of his flesh underneath her palm alerting her to the fact he was shirtless and wearing nothing but a pair of gray sweatpants that slung low on his hips. She resented the spark of arousal in her belly at the sight of the dark trail of hair disappearing under his waistband and hit him again.

Micah laughed at her, dodging the third blow she aimed at him. His hair was ruffled around his handsome face, his stubble dark on his jaw. He smelled of his soap, the sandalwood aftershave he used, and man. She let her eyes wander all over his body before returning to his face.

"You look rough," she said as he advanced on her, placing his palms against the door on each side of her face. He crowded her with his body, touching her with the lean muscles of his torso and the obvious erection straining against the soft cotton of his pants. Her heart sped up in her chest, and she took a couple of gulping breaths to steady her reaction to him and his obvious invitation.

"Do you have a problem with that?" Micah asked, his voice low and edged with desire and a touch of fatigue.

She grinned, shaking her head as she raised her own hands to skim his back and settle on his hips. "No, I don't have problem with it. I like it a little rough."

"I remember." Micah pressed his lips to hers with only the barest flicker of his tongue along her bottom lip before his grin caused her to pull back and glare at him.

"Is this a booty call? Is that your emergency?" She wanted her tone to carry more heat due to anger rather than her lust for him, but she knew she failed miserably. Deep down she didn't care why he called her; she was glad to see him, but she wasn't letting him off the hook so easily.

"I finished the book and all I could think about was telling you and celebrating."

Her heart did a wonky flip in her chest as an answering flush of lust spread over her skin. Micah did it for her, and the thought that he'd chosen her when he wanted someone to tell his news was absurdly romantic in her cynical mind. She fought the urge to go all mushy on him and opted for door number two: humor and an orgasm.

"And by celebrate you mean…"

"Peeling off your clothes and making you come."

He wasn't even pretending to be contrite, his grin making him look wicked and boyish at the same time. It was a combination guaranteed to make her do whatever he wanted. Bastard.

She gave up even the thin pretense of being mad and laughed, pulling him closer and wrapped her arms around his waist. Micah groaned a little and resumed the kiss, this time delving in deep and wet into her mouth, kissing her until they both had to surface for air.

"I missed you," Micah half-whispered into the space between them, and it caught her off guard, her heart thumping hard in her chest at the words. He cupped her cheek with his hand and rubbed his thumb over her bottom lip, dipping in a little for her to taste and suckle briefly.

"I missed you, too," she breathed against his chest, grateful for not having to look him in the eye when she said it. The words had popped out of her mouth before she engaged the keep-it-casual filter.

"Good." Micah stepped back and tugged her with him, spinning her so that he was guiding her backward into the bedroom area of the suite. He leaned in to kiss her, pushing her jacket off her shoulders, and she heard the whisper of fabric as it slid to the ground at their feet.

The bedroom area was bright with sunlight streaming through the floor-to-ceiling windows, but the heat of the day was nothing compared the fire in her belly as her desire spiked with each pass of her hands over his skin. She trailed her hands over his chest and pulled him down to her, taking his mouth this time in a kiss that communicated to Micah how much she wanted what he had to offer.

It had just been a few hours ago and she craved his touch, the way he made her feel. She knew he'd deliver on his promise to make her come, and she shivered in anticipation. His rough fingers brushing against her breast as he undid the buttons of her blouse was delicious. The cool air of the room against her exposed flesh as he tugged down the cups of her bra only increased her pleasure.

"I was writing the last scene, a sex scene, and all I could think about was tasting your nipples and you making that stuttery gasp sound." He dragged his thumb across the tip of her right breast, and she closed her eyes on her exhale. Micah half laughed and half growled. "Yeah, fuck, that one."

"Did you write us into a book?" she asked, shoving her hands underneath the waistband of his sweats and squeezing his ass. "Did you fuck me in your book?"

"Don't worry, I changed your name." Micah grinned, gently shoving Kelsey the last few steps into the bedroom. She stumbled back with a breathless laugh, pulling her blouse out her skirt and undoing the last few buttons and letting it hang open. "Even though I heard you screaming mine in my head."

"Well, come on and see if you can make it happen in real life and not just on the page," she said, watching his eyes turn black as his pupils dilated with his arousal.

Micah prowled toward her and she backed up the last few steps until her back was pressed against the glass of the window. She sucked in a breath when his fingers grasped the hem of her skirt and rucked it up until it pooled around her waist and she was exposed to the semi-rough fabric of his sweats against her skin, the sensual rub of his fingers against her inner thigh and the outside edge of her panties. The whimper that escaped past her lips was completely involuntary.

The phone in her pocket began to ring as one of Micah's long fingers slid under the edge of the silk lingerie and teased her wet flesh. Micah stopped his progress and growled in frustration.

"Do you have to answer it? Who is it?"

She recognized the ringtone as one of her fellow concierge staff. She reached up with a shaky hand and hit the button on her Bluetooth that would send the call to voicemail.

"Someone who can wait."

"Thank fuck," Micah groaned as he claimed her lips in a demanding kiss. Kelsey pushed aside any thoughts about the call now going to her inbox, the meeting with Babette... anything that wasn't Micah trailing his mouth down her chest toward her aching breasts.

The phone rang again, this time the ringtone for Perry. She cursed, filthy and vicious as her head thumped back against the glass.

Micah looked up at her from beneath his fringe of dark lashes. "Answer it. Don't mind me."

Kelsey wondered how she was going to ignore him, but she tapped the phone and answered. "Kyle."

Perry launched into a speech about some issue with the organizers of the convention, and she tried to concentrate as Micah trailed his mouth even closer to her breasts. He still watched her, and she couldn't pull her eyes away as his tongue circled her right nipple until it was wet and hard, and she was throbbing between her legs. She squeezed her thighs together and mirrored the action with her eyes, blocking out the carnal view in front of her.

"Yes, Perry, I'll take care of it. Not a problem," she said, working hard to modulate her voice and her breathing. It wasn't easy, and it got harder when Micah squeezed her left breast and rubbed the tip with his thumb in time with the continued movement of his tongue on its twin. She forced her eyes open and caught sight of Micah smoothing his hand down his rock-hard abdomen and into his sweats, his hand obviously tugging on his cock under the fabric. He glanced up, his eyes dancing with wicked laughter and a slow wink when he saw her watching.

Kelsey bit her lip against her own laughter, nothing in Perry's continued speech even remotely funny. She was never more grateful for hands-free calling when she reached out and slid her hand down into Micah's sweats and pushed his hand out of the way as she closed her fingers around his dick.

"I'll take care of it, Perry." She watched as Micah's eyes fluttered closed. "I have one…problem to take care of first."

"Yes, Perry," she said and pressed the button on her Bluetooth, whipping the device off her ear and tossing it over Micah's shoulder in the general vicinity of the bed. He hummed against her skin, his laughter at her frustrated movements easing into a low groan when she shoved at his sweats, pushing them down his thighs and allowing her full access to his body. Kelsey stroked him from root to tip, loving the way he bucked into her fist now wet with his pre-come.

She leaned up, kissing him hard on the mouth and dragging him closer to her body with a firm grip on his hip. "Hope you don't mind, but we have to make this quick."

"Whatever you need, baby." Micah wedged his body in close between her thighs and kissed everywhere he could reach while staying so close. She arched into it, wishing she had time to strip off her clothes and do this properly.

"A king-sized bed with 1800 thread-count sheets, and I'm going to let you fuck me with my ass pressed against the glass of the window," she said, not really complaining when his head dipped lower and he swirled her nipple with his tongue.

"But what a fine ass it is."

She was going to reply, but his long fingers delved underneath her panties and deep inside her body. She groaned, her head bashing against the window as he thrust in and out, the rhythm of his hand matching the pace of his mouth.

"You're so fucking wet," he murmured, adding his thumb to rub in a slow circle against her clit. Kelsey spread her legs wider, hiking one thigh around his waist to give him better access. "Oh yeah, you want it as much as I want to give it to you."

"Micah," she said panting against his cheek as he lifted his head and nuzzled her neck, licking and tasting the sensitive skin just below her ear. "I want this."

All morning she'd had to combat the way her mind drifted to last night, to the way he touched her, the way he held her when they finally fell into exhausted sleep. It had been a long time since she wanted anyone to stick around after the orgasms were done, but she loved the aftermath as much as she'd enjoyed the sex.

"Is this good?" he said against her skin as he continued his current movement inside her. "Or is this better?"

He shifted his angle, finding her G-spot and hitting it with every other thrust, giving her time to recover but edging her closer and closer to her release.

"Oh, there we go," he half moaned and half laughed as she bucked her hips in earnest against him, her body on autopilot as she raced all too soon for the finish line. Her lingerie was soaked, her thighs slippery from the arousal he demanded from her with every thrust, and she wanted to give it to him. She needed him to know what he did to her…even if she didn't want to dwell on that fact for too long in her own head. "Come on, Kelsey. Come on, baby. Give it to me now, and I swear I'll give you more later."

"Micah, please." She didn't even know she was speaking but the same words were rolling in loop in her brain as he picked up the pace, the pressure, and the deep strokes.

"Come on, baby." Micah pressed a soft kiss against her mouth, his tongue slipping in to tease as she cried out with each pulse of pleasure in her pussy. "Kelsey, please. I've got to feel you clench around my fingers. I'm dying here."

He was dying? She wanted to scoff but her body bowed with the impact of her orgasm slamming into her, and all she could was groan his name in his mouth as he kissed her hungrily. Kelsey gripped his shoulders, using him as an anchor to keep her body from sliding down the now warm, slick glass onto the floor.

"So good," she panted out as he continued his thrusting and drew out every single aftershock and wrung out every single drop of her pleasure. Mind numb. Body weak. She forgot everything but the rightness of being there with Micah Holmes.

"That's better," Micah growled against her ear, and she

choked out a wordless agreement as he buried his face against her neck. "If I didn't hear you come, I thought I was going to go mad."

Kelsey dragged her teeth across the skin of his exposed shoulder, her hand smoothing over the bare skin of his hip until she grasped his cock in her fist. Micah jumped, gasped, and then thrust into her grip, his body taut with his unresolved sexual need. Kelsey wanted him crazed under her mercy, like he'd done to her. She knew she had the power, and she'd used it last night and reveled in the head rush. She needed it now; craved it. Micah made her want things she should not want. Powerful things that could make her make stupid choices. On Sunday she'd get her sanity back, she'd go back to the old Kelsey, but for right now, she was giving in to the moment and the man.

"Let's see if I can make you lose your mind," she said and dropped to her knees.

...

Micah held his breath as Kelsey slid to her knees in between his legs.

She looked up at him, her hands roving over his chest, his belly, and his thighs as he closed his eyes and reveled in her touch. Anything she could give him, anything she would give him was enough. It was like he'd been in the desert on the horizon outside his window, and she was as sweet as water on his tongue.

He gazed down at her, time slowing down to a crawl as she wrapped her fingers around the base of his dick and gave him a long, slow pull. He thrust his hips forward and she met him halfway, licking the head of his cock and sucking it into her mouth. Micah cried out, no words, just a shout of pleasure at the heat and wet and the swirl of her tongue. He leaned forward, bracing his hands flat on the window. From this angle he could look down on her and not miss one wicked pass over her lips and into the depth of her mouth.

She would make him insane, and he'd love every minute of the fall into insanity.

He couldn't keep his hips still, but he didn't want to choke her, a good possibility considering the thin thread of control he had at this moment. Kelsey looked up at him, lifting off him as she continued to stroke him

"Come on, Micah," she said, her fingers digging harder into his hip as she licked his swollen head. "Make me take it."

The combination of her words and the slide of his shaft into her mouth compelled him to grant her wish. He shifted his hips, pushing in, pulling out. His eyelids fluttered as a wash of heat flooded over him, and her tongue did unspeakably wicked things to him.

"Come on. Do it," she mumbled, and his last bit of hesitation slid away as he leaned harder against the glass of the window, forcing her head back and keeping it in place with the angle. He thrust inside her mouth, forward with a snap of his hips and out with a long, slow glide. It was difficult, but he kept his eyes open, recording every debauched moment and storing it away for later.

"Oh fuck, Kelsey," Micah said. "Watching you take me…"

His climax was on him like a freight train, and he slapped his hand against the glass of the window as a full-body shudder wracked through him. A long, low groan was all he could manage as he thrust in time with the waves of his orgasm.

Flashes of light behind his eyelids. Rolling flashes of heat under his skin. A slice of pleasure so intense it was like ice going up and down his spine. He leaned his forehead against the window and huffed, catching his breath, and steadying his heart rate. Kelsey crawled up his body, kissing his hip, his belly, and finally his mouth as she dove in deep. Their combined tastes made his cock twitch against his thigh. A good idea, but not something he was going to achieve for a little while.

And Kelsey was a woman on the clock.

They clung to each other, boneless and blissed out as he drew her into a tight hug. It was passionate but also sweet with tenderness and easy companionship. With some women in the past this had been weird, the space between mindless passion and the quiet afterglow, but not Kelsey. It was just another extension of them and how well they synced up, and the realization made him want to slow down the time between now and Sunday. As if it could read his thoughts, the phone in her skirt pocket buzzed, and the big bad world intruded on their moment. Damn.

"Oh hell," she whispered against his neck, her arms tightening to keep him close. "I have to go. I don't want to go."

"I don't want you to go."

Long moments passed as they continued to stand there, ignoring the countdown of the clock. The phone buzzed again, and they both groaned and cursed.

"I think I have a panel soon," he said, glancing at his watch as he pulled his sweats up and over his hips, tying the drawstrings. Micah paused, watching Kelsey adjust her own clothes and regretting the need for her to cover up all that beautiful skin. "We could play hooky."

She cut him a look as she fastened the last of her buttons, taking the few steps necessary to close the distance between them. Kelsey pressed a quick kiss to his lips. "I would do it in a heartbeat, but my mortgage company really likes it when I pay them."

"Bastards."

"Bastards." She laughed and bent over to retrieve her Bluetooth earpiece from the floor. "I'll be at your panel and the dinner tonight."

"Please tell me Babette Forasch won't be at either event."

Kelsey froze, her hand stalled next to her ear. She recovered fast, but he saw a flash of apprehension on her features. He understood the reaction to the name. "I see you remember Babette."

"How could I forget her? She was the one who groped you at the fan event," Kelsey said. "She wasn't on the list for your dinner table tonight."

"Thank God. I don't know if I could keep my food down if she propositioned me for a threesome again."

Kelsey paused again as she fixed her hair in the mirror on his closet doors, meeting his eyes in the reflection. "She did what?"

"You heard me. She cornered me in the elevator this morning with her husband," he said, walking up behind her to loop his arms around her waist. "He likes to *watch*."

"He likes to…" She shook her head, her mouth opening and closing as she processed what he told her. "I knew she was a fan of yours but that's…"

"Yeah." Her phone buzzed again and he let her go, watching as she glanced at the screen. "Just keep her away from me until the convention is over. I'll warn you that I *will* throw you in her path if I see her coming."

He expected a laugh out of Kelsey, but all he got was a smile and another glance at her phone. Micah didn't need a neon sign to signal that she needed to go as much as he didn't want her to go.

"You need to take care of whatever is blowing up your phone, and I need to grab a shower and get ready for the panel." He grabbed her at the waist and guided her to the door, pressing a kiss to her neck before reaching for the door handle. "Thanks for answering my SOS."

Kelsey whirled in his arms, grabbing his face with both hands and kissed him with a sweet ferocity that surprised him. The kiss lingered, deep and simmering with heat until her phone buzzed again. They broke apart laughing at the interruption.

"I hate to come and run, but..." she said, reaching behind her for the door handle.

"Let's do it again," he said, trailing his fingers across her cheek. "More of the coming part and less of the running part."

"I'd like that," she said and slipped out of his room and into the hallway.

He tried to ignore just how much he liked it, too.

Chapter Fourteen

This was one of the weirdest things he'd ever been to in his life.

Micah stood beside "his" table at the dinner in the ballroom. The entire room was covered from top to bottom with lurid red and gold decorations. Hearts, big smoochy lips, photos with couples holding onto each other in an almost-kiss while in the ever-present windstorm, and nearly-hairless, naked cover model man chests visually assaulted him everywhere he turned.

He'd spent some time talking to the men earlier in the day at different workshops, and they were pretty great guys. Most of them had other jobs or owned their own businesses—usually in the fitness field—and they worked their asses off to get the biggest covers. He had no idea how they didn't freeze to death walking around shirtless in the subzero temperatures of the hotel, but he fought the urge to offer to buy them a sweater.

"Am I supposed to wax my chest? Is that a thing?" He leaned over to whisper in Kelsey's ear as she rearranged the goody bags at each place setting. Her skin was warm against his lips, and her spicy floral scent surrounded him. His mind immediately recalled damp skin, tangled sheets, and Kelsey wrapped around him. Damn. Micah shifted to make room for the way his cock reacted to the memory.

She snorted and gave him a narrow look over her shoulder. "Do you want to wax your chest? If you do, I've got a girl…"

Of course she did. She had somebody in this town to do everything. He laughed and backed up a couple of steps, reaching in his pants pocket to subtly adjust his erection. "I'm not saying that I want to do it. I don't think anyone in Bridger Gap waxes their chests…I can't say I've thought about it all that much."

She straightened up and looked him over, her assessment making him glance down to see what she saw. He was wearing a black suit with a crisp white shirt, and he left it open at the collar instead of wearing a tie. It had been Kelsey's suggestion so if she didn't like it, he was going to be no help with any other option. If it weren't for his sisters, he'd only have jeans and T-shirts in his closet.

She reached up and tugged on his lapel, smoothing her hand over the fabric before grasping his shirt collar and giving it a tug. Kelsey looked into his eyes, her full lips tilted with a hint of a smile. He matched her expression, exhaling deeply to settle the butterflies in his stomach. The girl gave him goddamn butterflies. She also made him hard and needy. Jesus.

She leaned in closer and pitched her voice so he could just hear it. "Personally, I like the way your chest hair rubs against my nipples when we're naked. It's hot."

He blinked, unable to stop the grin or the blush on his

cheeks. "So, no waxing for me."

"Good call," she said, running a fingertip along his neck before putting some distance between them. He would have said she was cool, that she wasn't as impacted by the heat they generated, but her hand shook a little when she reached up to tuck her hair behind her ear. Good to know.

"Your table guests were chosen by the convention organizers. They all requested your table and then there was some kind of lottery to see who will be here. They are true fans and excited to be here, so don't be nervous. Just let them talk, listen, and respond to what they say. It's okay to get them to talk about themselves if that's easier for you."

"Are you staying with me?" He hated that he sounded so needy, but the table was set up for him to have a plus one, and he liked how they worked the crowd together. She set him at ease and when he relaxed, he did fine.

"I can. My job is to be your go-to girl for this week."

A shout went up from over at the double doors that the event was on and they swung open and the rumble of sound wafting across the big room was like a train approaching from a distance getting closer and closer as the excited attendees spilled into the room.

"Smile, Micah. They already love you," Kelsey murmured as she walked forward to greet his first dinner guest. They spoke quietly for a couple of minutes, and then she turned to make the introductions.

"Micah, this Ellie and David Sewall."

"It's nice to meet you," he said, shaking David's hand and leaning down for Ellie to give him a kiss on the cheek. She didn't cling, so it was easy for him to pull back and get the space he needed.

"Mr. Holmes," Ellie said, her voice a little shaky.

"Call me Micah."

"Really?" she asked and looked at her husband with an

excited smile that made Micah relax. "Oh my God, you're my favorite author. I have books for you to sign, if you don't mind."

He glanced at Kelsey, who nodded and held up a Sharpie. Damn, she was perfect.

"You bet, Ellie. I'd love to." She was dressed up for a fancy dinner, and her husband was wearing a flight suit. It was clearly a costume, and Micah had no idea why he was dressed that way. "Great costume."

David nodded in thanks and cast a tolerant but loving glance at his wife. "It's that guy from your book about the pilot who crashes and everybody thinks he's dead. I've never read it but it's her favorite, and she wanted me to dress like him."

"You're a good husband, man."

"Thanks for not writing about a ballet dancer or something because there was no way in hell I was wearing tights."

He laughed, placing a hand on his shoulder in solidarity when Kelsey interrupted them with another couple. Well, a lady and her...blow up doll.

"Micah, this Sarah and..." Kelsey trailed off, looking at a complete loss for the first time since he'd known her. He didn't blame her.

The newest guest smiled and hoisted her doll further up on her hip. "I don't have a date, so I made my own. He's Caleb Mattwell from *Safe Harbor*. I love that book so much."

"That's awesome, Sarah. Thank you."

He reached out to squeeze her hand in thanks, and she clung to him, her fingers damp and shaking just a little bit with the emotion also pooling in her eyes. She blinked hard, forcing back the tears that clearly threatened her smile. He braced himself for her story, glancing over to Kelsey for reinforcement. She smiled at him, giving him a little "go ahead" motion.

"I lost my husband, and your books helped me while I sat at hospice with him."

"I'm really sorry for your loss, Sarah." He squeezed her hand, letting her know that he was listening, ready to hear whatever she needed to say. "Tell me about your husband."

"Ned was a lot like Caleb," she said. "Strong and quiet and really sweet, but with enough of the bad boy to keep it interesting."

Micah chuckled when she waggled her eyebrows, and she did too, her own laugh clogged with the weight of her emotions.

"Your books, all your books, were like the love we shared, and now that he's gone I can read them and remember. I can dive into your books, and it takes me back to when Ned and I met and fell in love."

Micah had listened to something similar from other fans in other towns a million times before, but this time he *heard* her. He heard the meaning his books—his words—had on her life, and he was humbled by it.

He cleared his throat of the emotion clogging it. He glanced at Kelsey who was watching him closely. She was close enough to hear the conversation and she cocked her head at him, clearly wondering what he might do. But he didn't need her coaching tonight; this one was pure instinct.

"Sarah, I don't have a date for tonight. Would you like to be my date?"

Her eyes flew open, and she slapped a shaky hand over her mouth, nodding with frantic enthusiasm.

"Yeah? Is that a yes?" he asked, grabbing the inflated doll and handed it off to Kelsey who gave him a discreet thumbs-up. He returned his attention to Sarah, guiding her over to the table. "Come on over. I think we're going to have a great time tonight."

To his surprise, they did have a good time. His dinner

companions were all friendly and fun and very relaxed after the initial awkwardness wore off, and the time flew by. Kelsey sat across the table with the blow-up doll, giving him a smile that told him he wasn't fucking this up.

Her approval meant a lot to him, and he wasn't so quick to push it away like he had before. They were a great team, in and out of bed. There was a reason why she'd been the first person he wanted to tell earlier when he finished the book. It was the same reason he kept seeing Sunday on his horizon like a big, red-flashing beacon that kept getting closer and closer. He just hadn't decided if he was going to do anything about it or not. Kelsey was hard to read and every time he thought about bringing it up, he chickened out.

He was saying good-bye to Sarah, Ellie, David, and his other guests when Kelsey took a phone call and wandered away from the chatter of the table. His attention was torn between the good-byes and the expression of concern on her face as she exited the ballroom and headed toward the lobby.

Micah waved a final good-bye, only blushing a little when Sarah pressed a kiss to his cheek before he headed off to look for Kelsey. He found her walking toward him across the lobby, her expression still clouded by concern.

"Are you okay?" He reached out, cupping her face with his hand as he leaned in closer to hear her over the din in the vast open space of the hotel. People's voices rumbled, raucous laughter, and the ever-present electronic noise of slot machines filled the air.

He knew he should step back. They were in full-view of the other guests and the hotel staff, and his actions could get Kelsey in trouble, but he didn't care. She was clearly upset, and his only thought was to see what he could do to make it right for her.

"I have to go. The nursing facility called about my mom." She looked down at the phone in her hand and he saw it for what it was, the time for her to compose herself. He gave her the time, and when she looked up he acted like he didn't see the tremble in her bottom lip. "She had a bad night and my dad is on duty for a while." She looked up at the ceiling, her voice betraying her frustration. "I need to go. I'm sorry about tonight…"

He cut her off with a hug, his arms wrapped tightly around her until he felt some of her tension ease away from her body. Micah debated his immediate reaction to her words, knowing that following his instinct would definitely cross the line that existed between two people who were parting company in a couple of days. What the hell. He was in Vegas, and if he was ever going to gamble, this was the place.

"Can I go with you?"

Kelsey pulled back. "I can't ask you do that."

"You didn't." He tucked a strand of hair behind her ear. "If we get there and you don't need me, I'll take off."

She started shaking her head, and he cut her off, not really wanting to accept no for an answer. Yeah, they were having fun, but he liked her. They connected, and he really needed to do this for her.

"Look, you've helped me out way beyond your job, and I'd like to return the favor." He nudged her with his elbow. "I'm more than a pretty face and a big penis."

Kelsey laughed at that, and the clench of tension in his belly released. God, the look of stress on her face when she talked about her mom had not sat well with him at all. He was a fixer, he liked to actively tackle things and do what he could to make them right. It was why he joined the Marines and also why he loved to write. On the page he was the master and commander, and his actions mattered. He liked to take care of the people in his life as well, and right now that included Kelsey.

"I'd like it if you went with me." She nodded as if to

convince herself as she spoke the words. "Please."

"I'll meet you in the same spot with your car, I need to run up to my room to get something, okay?"

She nodded, and he subdued the urge to kiss her on the lips. They were in the lobby, and while a concerned pat on the back or a hug could be explained away, his lips on any part of her anatomy would require a lot of explaining.

He settled for a squeeze of her hand, watching as she walked in the direction of the staff area of the hotel knowing that the ache in the vicinity of his heart wouldn't go away until he saw her again.

•••

Desert Rest Nursing facility was a good place.

Kelsey led the way as they navigated the too-familiar halls, past the quiet of the patient rooms and the subdued activity at the nursing stations. Many of the staff nodded and smiled at her their eyes shining with their ever-present sympathy that she had to be here. Her mom was young to have dementia, and the folks around here appreciated the tragedy of it all.

"This is very nice," Micah said as he kept pace with her down the corridor. He'd come down to her car on the street still in his suit but carrying the messenger bag he now had draped across his chest. His big hand was around her own, giving her silent support and needed warmth as she fought off the chill of the air-conditioned building.

"It is. With my dad and I both working, we can afford to pay for her residency. The staff is excellent, and they're experts in dealing with people with dementia. We spent a lot of time looking around and this was the best, and we were lucky to get her here."

"I would guess that to know she was with the best makes it a little easier to leave her here."

"You have no idea, and I hope you never do." Her words were clipped, but hopefully full of the sincerity behind them. She really wouldn't wish this on anyone.

She could make the last turn with her eyes closed, several visits each week had made her intimately familiar with every scuff on the wall, every flower in the pretty wallpaper border, and every blip and beep from the sundry medical equipment lining the rooms and hallways. She didn't even smell the antiseptic odor anymore; it was now part of the landscape of her life.

Her mother's door was closed, and she pushed down on the lever gently, hoping that she was asleep and scared to wake her if she was. It usually took her mom quite awhile to come down after she had an episode, even though you'd think the physical outburst and emotional ups and downs would wear her out. They didn't like to drug the patients here if they could let them calm down naturally, and that was one of the things that drew Kelsey and her father to Desert Rest. It was bad enough that her mother was a shadow of what she had been without reducing her to a drugged-out mess.

Her mom was sitting up in bed, her fingers plucking at the covers, chattering randomly and far too quickly to be understood. Sylvia, one of the night nurses, sat by her bed, stroking her mother's arm as she made soothing sounds. She looked up as Kelsey entered the room and smiled, only a slight twist to her mouth betraying her regret at the situation.

"Kelsey, she's doing much better. You didn't need to come down."

"I know, but you knew I would."

"That I did." She rose from her chair, her curious gaze looking at where Micah stood by her side, her eyes not missing their joined hands.

"Sylvia, this my friend, Micah Holmes."

"The author?" The nurse's eyebrows rose in surprise.

"Your mom will be excited to meet him, I bet." She directed her next comment to Micah with a wave of her hand at the bookshelves covering one of the walls and full of books. "You're one of her favorites. I was just going to read to her, try to get her to go back to sleep."

Micah cleared his throat next her and Kelsey turned as he dropped her hand, reaching into his bag and pulling out a large stack of paper, secured with an oversize rubber band.

"I remembered you telling me that she liked to have people read to her." His cheeks and necks darkened a little with his next words. "I brought my new book. I thought I could read to her if that's okay…"

His voice trailed off as she reached up and hugged him hard around the neck.

"Jesus, Micah Holmes. Stop being…"

"Being what?" His arms came around her, the one holding the book against her back the other cupping her head, and he pressed a kiss to her temple. "Stop being awesome? Sorry, I can't do that."

She laughed, wiping at her eyes with the back of one hand and smacking him lightly on the chest with the other. She was never going to tell him the rest of that sentence. He was leaving on Sunday and so those words—amazing, kind, terrific in bed, funny, smart, sweet—those words would go to her grave.

"Yeah, yeah," she said, looking up at him and loving the way his smile carried that edge of wicked. "So, Mr. Awesome, you want to meet my mom?"

"I'd like that."

Sylvia nodded at them both as she exited the room, and Kelsey made a mental note to get her and the other staff a fruit basket or something for everything they did so well. She turned to the woman on the bed who still looked like the same person who'd tucked her into bed, helped her with algebra, bought her a dress for prom, and laughed and cried with her as the moment required. Now that woman was gone, and it was a challenge every day for Kelsey to reconcile the memories she carried deep in her heart and the woman who was here now.

"Mama, it's Kelsey." She sat on the edge of the bed, reaching out to touch her mother's hand, giving it a soft stroke to help soothe her. "It's Kelsey."

"I don't know you," her mother said, her voice firm but also shaky on the edges.

"Yeah, you do. It's Kelsey. I bring you the books. I read to you, and brush your hair." She reached up and touched the tangled strand sitting on her mother's shoulder. "It's Kelsey."

"Kelsey." Her mother's face softened, the tone of confusion easing as she nodded. She didn't fool herself that she remembered who she was, remembered that she even had a daughter—her father was the only one who had breakthroughs at this point—but she knew her as her reading buddy, and that was enough. "You're Kelsey."

"This is my friend Micah." She turned to look at the man standing over her shoulder, his gentle smile calming her nerves and making this whole thing seem *right*. "Micah, this is my mom, Caroline Kyle."

He stepped forward, easing down into the chair next to bed and lowering his voice as if he knew that his height and a loud voice might not help this situation. Micah was good at things like that, knowing what to do at the right time, like he'd done tonight with Sarah. He got so wrapped up in the frantic emotions of his fans, his frustration about not getting to write what he wanted that he failed to trust his instincts and stumbled through appearances.

The real Micah would be a dangerous man if he ever figured out the power he held in his smile and his natural demeanor. She'd fallen for it, and she was a tough crowd to sell to.

"It's nice to meet you, Mrs. Kyle." Her mother shied away from him, edging behind Kelsey a little, only giving a slight nod to acknowledge his presence. Undeterred, Micah continued. "Kelsey tells me you like to read romance novels. I'd like to read to you, if that's okay."

Kelsey turned back to look at her mom. "I think that would be fun, Mom. I'll brush your hair while he does it. Is that okay?"

Her mother nodded, and Micah said, "Thank you, Mrs. Kyle. This is a new one, so I hope you like it."

Kelsey moved around to the opposite side of the bed, picking up the brush and settling in behind her mom as Micah began his reading of the book in his hands. His voice was low, deep and the southern drawl made the entire experience a delight. She'd never tell Aiden, but Micah could do the audio on his own books and women would buy them just to hear his dark-honey voice talk dirty to them.

The whole thing mesmerized her mom, and as she brushed her hair, she could feel and see the tension leaving her body. Kelsey brushed through her curls for an hour, listening as Micah spun out a story that had her riveted from the first page. It soothed her as much as it did her mom, his talent for writing the words that resonated deep inside every heart delivering the perfect gift. If she had any say in the matter, and she didn't fool herself for a minute that she did, she would tell Micah to keep doing this even if he had to branch out into another genre. There had to be room for him to do both.

Her mom slid down under the covers as her relaxation drifted into sleep, and a quick glance at the clock told Kelsey that it was just after midnight. Micah kept reading, waiting until she tucked the duvet around her mom to stop.

As if he could read her mind, Micah tucked away the book in his bag and followed her out into the hallway. He said nothing as she nodded her good-bye to the nurses and they made their way out of the building and into the cooler night air. The sky was bright with the distant neon and glitter, but in the far distance she could see the stars twinkling in the dark of the night. He took her keys from her, and she let him sliding into the passenger seat and watching those distant spheres of gas and fire, making the same wish she'd made since her mother's diagnosis.

Micah let her remain in her own thoughts, and she was grateful for the reprieve from conversation. It was always so tough after seeing her mom, and she needed time to get her headspace right. Before she knew it, he pulled her car onto the street around the corner from the hotel as a safeguard against being spotted by a co-worker. He parked but didn't cut the engine, the hum and constant bellow of Las Vegas traffic their soundtrack.

"You look so much like her, you know," he said, his voice barely above a whisper. "Two of the most beautiful women I've ever seen."

Kelsey looked over at him, smiling her thanks. "She still looks the same. It's what makes this so hard sometimes. I look at her, and I see my mom. I see her, and it kills me that she doesn't see me back." She inhaled and exhaled slowly. "Thank you so much for tonight."

Her voice caught on the solid lump of emotion wedged in her throat, and she swallowed hard blinking back the pain that prickled in her eyes and lower in her chest. She didn't want to cry. Tears had been shed and had changed nothing. There was nothing her grief or anger or despair could do to change any of this hell. It didn't stop the tears from escaping and running down her cheeks faster than she could wipe them away.

"Hey," Micah said, moving over and dragging her to him. She went willingly, needing the comfort he gave her. Rock solid. Dependable. Caring. Micah was the kind of guy you kept and not the kind you put on a plane and filed away as a great memory.

And fuck did she want to keep him. Or crazier still... go with him. The only thing that could cut through the ache caused by another visit to her mom was the panic that shot along her veins when the importance of her thought caught up in her brain. Go with him? Oh no. That was...nuts and exactly what she wanted. Not a place, she didn't even care where—she just wanted him and a chance to be together and ride this out. Her fingers were numb from the shock-induced cold when she pushed away from him, disguising the tremor by tucking her hair behind her ears.

"You all right, Kelsey?" Micah stared at her, his gaze armor-piercing in its intensity. "Baby, you okay?"

She nodded, hoping her voice really sounded as confident as she tried to project. "I'm tired. I think I should go."

"Sure." The one word answer didn't hide his disappointment, but he reached for the door handle, shifting in the seat as if he was going to exit until he stopped, paused, and then spoke. "We've got tonight, and tomorrow night, and I don't care if all we do is sleep in the same bed, but I'd like to spend tonight with you."

Oh man, the devil wasn't wearing pitchforks and horns. Nope, that was all Halloween hype. The real deal was disguised as the desire you wanted so deep down that you might not even dare to speak it to yourself.

"I don't think so. I need... Tonight, I think I need to be alone."

He didn't turn around, only nodded and pulled the door handle and levered his long body out of her tin car. She exited on her side and their gazes met over the roof of the vehicle, his gorgeous face lit up with the glow of the bright neon from the strip club across the street.

"Call if you need me." He paused and glanced down,

shaking his head. "If you need anything."

She didn't miss the precise word use, understanding that he also knew what a precipice they were on.

"Thanks…again…for everything."

He nodded and slapped the top of the car, slipping her a cocky grin as he turned and moved around the car and stepped up on the sidewalk. He walked backward for a while, his eyes never leaving her face until the turn at the corner forced him to turn around and disappear from her view.

Kelsey got in her car, and put her hands on the steering wheel as she huffed out a breath that should have been steadying, but only amped up the mixed up feelings pinging around in her head. She'd go for a drive in the desert and clear her head. Or she could go home and find Sarina or Aiden or Lilah and have drinks and laughs and maybe a dip in the pool, back-to-normal things with her friends and a break from the fantasy world centered on Micah.

She looked over shoulder, pulled into the early morning traffic, and pointed her car toward home. Kelsey had no idea how she ended up in the employee section of the hotel parking garage and on the elevator to the lobby and then to the fortieth floor. All she did know was that her heart pounded in her chest and blood rushed through her veins, the sound deep in her ears almost drowning out the sound of her knuckles rapping on the large, wooden door in front her. It slid open, and there he was, Micah, with rumpled hair, eyeglasses, barefoot, shirtless with only the suit pants from earlier still on. His confusion swiftly morphed into delight, desire, and longing, the combination enough to loosen her tongue.

"I changed my mind. Can I stay here with you?"

Chapter Fifteen

For a man who made his living by stringing words together, he had none.

Micah stared at Kelsey, blinking to clear his head and recall that she could not stand in his hallway. It was risky for her, for her job. He reached a hand out and tugged her inside, shutting the door behind them.

He'd left her on the sidewalk, and it had taken everything in him not to turn around and try harder to change her mind. He wanted Kelsey, wanted her for more than a few days, but she wasn't a woman you pushed. The wrong move and she'd run, and he'd never get a second chance. But here she was, and he wasn't going to waste time worrying about a tomorrow he wanted and would never get. He'd take what he could have for tonight because their clock was winding down to the final hour. On Sunday he would go home, and she would stay here. Done. Over. Finished.

He finally found his voice. "I was hoping you'd change your mind." Micah pulled her close, wrapping his arms around her waist, loving the way her body fit against his own. "I've dreamed about having you here."

"How do you do that?" she asked, her arms rising to loop around his neck, her fingers twisting in his hair and softly stroking is neck.

"How do I do what?"

"Make me feel…" Kelsey trailed off, her mouth twisting a little as she pondered her words. "You make me feel."

"I know what you mean," he said, smiling when a blush spread across her cheeks. They both laughed, and it was the same between them again, as easy and intense as it had from the start.

Kelsey leaned up and gave him a gentle kiss, supping at his lips until he parted them. Her hands gripped Micah's shoulders before sliding down his chest, her palms stroking his muscles underneath the soft material of his T-shirt, and then slid around his waist to hug him close. Micah gave her a gentle tug, turning and walking her backward toward the bed, determined to lay her down on the king-size bed, strip her down to nothing but skin, and love her all night long.

Kelsey pulled back from their kiss and pulled off her blouse, tossing it to the floor, her skirt joining it before she slid her hands into his waistband and helped him to remove his pants. Two soft thuds and her heels were gone, and she eased onto the mattress lifting her hand to encourage him to join her. He did, making sure every inch of his skin rubbed along hers until they were face-to-face.

"You fucking make me want so much," he whispered against Kelsey's lips. He had never felt this level of heat and need for another person. Kelsey was stunning when she was passionate about something. Whether it was her favorite club or the way she arched into his touch, she brought 100 percent to the table and that was exciting, captivating. He knew she held back her heart and her future, but it didn't diminish the excitement of being with her now. It made it quite the opposite because he found himself wanting to breach those barriers and make her *want* as well.

Micah knew there would never be anyone else for him after this week in Las Vegas. He wanted Kelsey to feel that too, to know it deep in her gut both physically and emotionally.

"I want to fuck you. All night. I want to own you. Have you," he growled against her lips.

"Then do it. It's why I came back. I need you."

He slid his hand into Kelsey's hair, wrapping her curls around his fingers and using the grip to pull her head back, to allow him to kiss her harder, deeper. Kelsey's mouth was yielding, lips soft, and surrendered as he drove the kiss. Their limbs tangled together, and when he shifted to get even closer, she broke off the kiss with a gasp as he rocked their groins together, sliding his hard cock along the swollen folds of her pussy. Micah groaned as Kelsey wrapped her legs around. He pushed his body up, braced one arm over her, memorizing the look of her laid out before him: naked, wanting, open.

"I need you," Kelsey said, pulling Micah back close against her warm, silky skin. Micah lifted her hand and pressed soft kisses against her fingers, her palm, and then the pulse pounding at her wrist. Finally, Micah slid his fingers between Kelsey's as he leaned over and kissed her. He had to raise himself up on his knees to get in closer, and Kelsey spread her legs wider, silently urging him to take what he wanted.

A wave of possession and hunger raced through Micah as he broke off the kiss and looked down at his lover. Running his palms over her skin, down the toned length of her body, he cupped her breasts, caressing her tight nipples with his fingertips until she closed her eyes and writhed under his touch.

"Please, Micah."

"Please what?" he said, leaning over to lightly suck on a nipple.

"I need to come," she moaned, writhing underneath his attention.

"I'll get you there, baby. Be patient."

Kelsey growled beneath him, her nails digging into his shoulder and betraying her true frustration.

Micah lifted his head and settled in closer between her thighs, rubbing his cock against her core with a groan of his own. She felt so fucking good. It felt *right* between them. Kelsey shifted her legs further apart, making room for Micah and sliding her hands over his shoulders and his back, as if she needed to touch every available part of him.

Micah gripped the back of her thigh, pulling it higher on his hip as he kissed her, slowly sliding his tongue against hers. He wanted them to take their time, have the chance to taste and feel and indulge in each other before they lost all self-control.

Kelsey sighed against his mouth, her fingers digging into his ass cheeks and drawing her in closer.

"I've wanted this. I've wanted…" Kelsey said.

"You've never had this?" Micah asked.

"Not this," Kelsey answered. "I haven't had this."

Micah brushed his lips against her cheek, nodding in understanding. "We have it now. Together."

She nodded and looped a hand around his neck, pulling him down to her and into a demanding kiss. Kelsey wrapped her arms around him even tighter, shifting under his body to angle their connection to get more friction between them. She lifted her hips, arching to rub her clit against his cock, and Micah groaned appreciatively, his hand sliding up Kelsey's leg to grip and pull at her hip. He lifted off her, shifting back on his heels to reach into his side drawer and grab a condom.

Kelsey watched him sliding her own hand down her belly to caress her sex. The view made his hands shake, increasing the imperative to be inside her tonight. He caught her wicked smile but didn't let it stop him from reaching down and grabbing her hand, pressing it on the mattress next to the silken fall of her hair.

"Don't start without me."

"Stop playing around, and get inside me, Micah."

"Nobody wants that more than me right now, baby."

He rolled on the condom and then crawled back up between Kelsey's legs. His hands slid over her body again, soaking in the heat of her skin, lingering over the spot in the crease of her thigh that was highly sensitive. He leaned over, kissing her stomach and further up until he took a turn at each of her breasts. Her nipples were sweet, tight and the sound she made when he suckled made his cock harden to the point of aroused pain.

"Fuck, Kelsey," he hissed as he lifted up to nip at her lips.

"Yes, please," Kelsey nodded and he couldn't help but grin at her, the answering smile on her own lips ratcheting the heat between them even higher.

Kelsey's hands dragged down Micah's body and he stilled, enjoying the roaming caress of her touch. He ran fingertips along the inside of her thigh, compelled to touch, to explore. Soaking in the way she writhed underneath him, her hands fisting in the sheets when he ducked his head to kiss the spot he'd been stroking.

"Please, Micah. Now."

The obscene ache in her voice made him shudder and he inched even closer, lining his cock up at the entrance to her pussy. He gripped his erection in his fist, rubbing it against her folds, getting slicked up with her own lube. They stared at each other as he poised above her, desperate to slide into her tight, slick sheath.

"Hang on, baby. This is going to take a while."

...

She needed him now. Right now.

Kelsey swallowed hard and reached for Micah, her grip closing around his cock. Micah flexed his hips, shoving in her hand, his eyes locked on the sight. She lingered over her caress, stroking the shaft, and skimming over the head and then dragging her fingers against Micah's balls.

"Kelsey, I need you."

Oh that was so good to hear because she felt like she was drowning in her own want, sinking into a riptide that she was powerless to resist. Micah removed both their hands and pushed up to his knees and kissed her, taking his time. She wanted this to go fast, but she enjoyed and soaked in the last few moments of anticipation. Their eyes locked, Micah reached down between them and pushed himself into her body.

She lifted her hips, gasping as the slick head of his cock slipped inside and one long push seated him balls deep in her body. She reached out, gripping his hip and pulling him even closer, even though it was impossible.

Micah lowered his body onto hers, brushing his nose against her cheek as he flexed his hips and pushed deeper into her. The shift of his body against hers, the rub of his cock against her clit, Micah's groan made her shudder as he pulled out and then filled her up.

His sigh was warm against her cheek as she started to moan. Micah lifted his head and kissed her hungrily, desperately, weaving his fingers into her hair, slowly rocking his hips against her. He promised to make this last as long as possible.

Kelsey followed his lead, joining in the slow, rocking motion as their tongues slid together, and she wrapped her arms around Micah's neck to hold him close, to anchor herself to him as her world spiraled out of control. They'd done this fast and hectic, hard and heavy but this was slow and sensual.

It was everything decadent, gasping breath and the wet, deep slide of their kisses.

"I have to move. Harder," Micah said against her throat, his chest heaving with his effort. Kelsey lifted her knee higher, gasping when it pulled Micah deeper inside her.

Micah groaned, fingers digging into her hip as he pulled back and thrust in with the full power of their passion.

Kelsey shivered under him. "Please, baby, move. Harder. Now."

He kissed her again, and she enjoyed the continued slow, even thrusts of their lovemaking and the slow slide of their bodies rather than trying to reach the end too soon. Kelsey tightened her grip on his arm, moaning with each thrust. She loved each time he pulled out and then pushed back in, touching all the parts inside her that made her toes curl.

"Fuck, Kelsey," Micah whispered as he pressed his face against her neck. Their bodies rocked with languid rhythm, and she followed his lead. Micah leaned up and captured her mouth as he picked up the rhythm, matching it with his tongue against her own.

Micah sank into the kiss for a few more seconds before pushing himself up with both hands and looming over her. He gripped Kelsey's hips and pulled her back on his cock, fucking into her with each pull. Micah's hands roamed over her body as he rolled his hips.

"Fuck. Please," he said, his voice heavy with arousal. He was gorgeous, the pleasure of the moment written over every taut muscle, each inch of silky skin. The sheets rustled and she tightened her thighs around his hips as he fucked her, slowly.

Kelsey watched his expression as he stared down at the sight of his cock pushing into her pussy, and she could not look away. His grip on her hip tightened just as he looked up to meet her eyes. She whispered his name, and he bent over to kiss her deeply and roughly. Instead of the kiss slowing him down, he snapped his hips faster, harder into her body, and Kelsey bucked under him, begging for more. Kelsey cried out into his mouth and Micah pulled back, and she fought back the urge to hide all the feelings she usually tried to conceal: pleasure, longing, urgency, and need.

"This is what I want from you, baby," Micah said. "Everything."

She swallowed hard, forcing the words out between gasps. "I'd give it you."

"I'll take it," he whispered. "I'll take everything you'll give me."

Micah picked up the strength of his thrusts, joining her gasps and moans as he drove them both closer to orgasm. His cock was hard, stroking in deep, and she arched upward, crying out.

"I'm coming, Micah. Yes."

The pleasure was white-hot and her skin caught fire as the orgasm raced through her. She kept pushing back against him, craving him deeper inside her with each thrust. She wanted to crawl inside him, to keep him inside her, to remain with him in this moment for as long as she could.

Both of them were damp with sweat even though the room was chilly, everywhere his skin touched hers was on fire. Micah's movements became sharper, harder, desperate as he chased his own pleasure, and she could not take her eyes off his face. He was wide open, hardened with his need. She would never get tired of watching him fuck her, his entire being invested in the act of them enjoying each other in the best way. Micah did nothing halfway, and she was helpless to do anything but follow him into the frenzy.

"Baby," he groaned in a crazed voice as he laid himself out over Kelsey again and pressed his forehead against her own. He fucked her hard and fast, and she dragged her nails down his back until Micah reached out and took her hands in his own. He entwined their fingers together, and she cherished the gesture as he rocked into her and rode her into his climax.

Their damp bodies slapped together, hands clasped tightly as he threw his head back and cried out. His body was taut, covered in a sheen of sweat, his neck strained with the hoarse roar of his pleasure. He was gorgeous, and she didn't want to let him go. She didn't have time to be afraid of her thoughts, not with Micah sweetly kissing her lips, her cheeks, her sweat-dampened hair.

"I don't have to go back to Georgia on Sunday, Kelsey," Micah whispered, his arms wrapping around her body as he held her close.

Her breath caught as she waited. Waited for the panic. Waited for the knee-jerk reaction to make a joke of his suggestion. But she didn't want to do any of those things. She wanted this to be different. She wanted it to be different with Micah.

This was the last moment to stop this train, to make the choice to open herself up to this man or to stay in the place she carved out for herself out of necessity and self-protection. She would make her heart vulnerable again for the first time in a long time and was also giving up a chance to guarantee her career advancement.

Her head was running the numbers, counting the cards on the table, but her heart…her heart was shoving the stack of chips to the middle and making a bet.

"Stay," she whispered in his ear.

He pulled back and looked down at her, his smile tentative and hopeful, and it made her heart kick up even higher.

"Yeah?" he asked.

"Yeah," she nodded. "As your concierge I can change your reservation."

Chapter Sixteen

Getting fired wasn't the worst thing about her current situation.

She was standing in Perry's office, wearing the same clothes she'd worn the day before and smelling of sex and Micah's aftershave—not her finest professional moment, but that wasn't the worst part of this scenario. No. That was the smug look Babette Forasch was leveling at her from across the room.

Years of professional behavior. Years of following the rules of the hotel and her own personal code. Years of working toward her goal of management within the company. All that time and hard work down the big toilet of her life because she gave in to her heart and got caught by a tacky trophy wife as she was making her (supposedly discreet) walk of shame at the ass crack of dawn.

Fuck her.

Perry leaned against his desk, his arms crossed over his chest. The frown on his face was epically cold and told her that if she didn't have a damn fine excuse, then he was going to personally escort her out of the building with her personal items packed up in a box.

"Ms. Kyle, Mrs. Forasch has made a serious accusation, namely that you violated the no-fraternization rule here at the hotel by engaging in a sexual relationship with a guest."

"She is screwing Micah Holmes," Babette whined from across the room. Her husband's hand on her arm stopped her from saying whatever else was on her mind.

"Ms. Kyle, do you have anything to say?" Perry asked, his expression grim, but she saw a flicker of something else in his eyes—sympathy, disappointment. "If this is a case of misunderstanding or mistake, I'm sure we can clear it up."

He needed to get in line if he thought he had the market cornered on that emotion. She'd done this to herself and had no one else to blame. Kelsey knew how this was going to end—she would be fired, and no high-end hotel in town would touch her with a ten-foot pole when the "why" of her termination got out. The hotelier community in Vegas was small, and she had zero chance to keep this under wraps. She didn't know how she was going to pay the mortgage and her share of the bill for her mother.

This was a fucking disaster.

She could lie but that wasn't her style. She might have been a rule breaker, but she wasn't a liar. It would be cold comfort when she was unemployed but at least she'd be able to look herself in the eye.

"It's not a mistake." The words weren't easy to say, but she made sure that her voice did not waiver. She wouldn't give Babette the satisfaction.

"Ms. Kyle." Perry dragged her name out on a long sigh as he dipped his head to his chest and looked down at his feet.

"I don't have to remind you that sleeping with a guest means that you will be fired. Do you want to re-think that answer?"

Kelsey stared at him. Was he asking her to lie?

"Kelsey." Saul Forasch spoke up from across the room, his tone the usual level of sleazy that made her skin crawl. Whatever he was going to say, she knew she wasn't going to like it. "My only interest in this is getting my wife what she wants, and that is one-on-one time with Micah Holmes."

"I know what kind of one-on-one time she wants with Micah."

"Kyle," Perry's voice carried a warning. She wasn't stupid and shut her mouth. Anything else along these lines would sound jealous and petty. Not far from the truth but not something she was going to share with the class.

"If you can arrange to get Babette what she originally requested, then I'm sure I can speak to the management and ensure you keep your job and get the trainee spot," Saul said.

She stared at him, never doubting he could make it happen. He was dangling the most delicious carrot in front of her, and damn, but it was tempting. But…no.

Micah didn't want to do it, and after his last encounter with Babette in the elevator, he wouldn't do it. But the bottom line is that she didn't want to ask him.

"I'm sorry, Mr. Forasch, but I can't do it. Mr. Holmes is very clear that he is not interested, and I have to respect it."

"You just want to keep him for yourself." Babette pouted, every word laced with spite. Kelsey let her anger flare at this entire situation. It was aimed at Babette, herself…but mostly at herself.

"You bet I do," she said, ignoring the sharp look shot at her by Perry. "You'll have my resignation within the hour."

Kelsey walked out of the office, shoving the glass doors open and moving quickly across the lobby to the elevators. She wanted to get to Micah before Perry sent hotel security after her and escorted her out of the hotel for good. Kelsey needed to get to Micah and explain about Babette before he heard it from someone else, before it drove a wedge between them and shattered what they'd begun just last night. They hadn't spoken the words, but she knew she was in love with Micah Holmes. Not falling...she'd taken the tumble and landed in a tangle of emotions and hope and longing after the free fall.

Last night she'd learned she wasn't alone. At the end Micah was there with her, and he would help her get through this. While her life was a mess right now, unemployment, her professional reputation in tatters, the jeopardy of her mom's care all bearing down on her like a freight train with no breaks, it was bearable because Micah was with her.

Loyal, loving Micah who'd captured her the moment he'd invited her into his suite.

She hurriedly pressed the button to call the elevator, stepping inside and swiping her card for access to his floor, hoping they hadn't already cancelled her access. She exhaled on a prayer of thanks when the doors closed and began the ascent to the fortieth floor. Luckily, it was early in the morning, so there were no stops on interim floors and within a minute she was stepping into the hallway and headed for her lover's door. Two heavy knocks and she steeled herself to not fall apart the minute he opened the door.

She lasted three minutes.

One minute a sleepy, sex-rumpled Micah was opening the door and the next she was in his arms, trying not to fall to pieces and failing miserably. The tears that had stung her eyes and the back of her throat since the confrontation with Babette in Perry's office spilled out and over her cheeks and onto his bare chest.

His arms circled her immediately and she sank into them, wondering how she'd gone the last two hours without feeling his touch. She craved him, needed him. Three days was all it had taken to turn her whole goddamn world upside down and have no regrets. Three days.

"Hey, baby. Kelsey?" Micah's lips brushed against her temple, his words a whisper against her skin. "Are you okay? Is it your mom?"

She shook her head, allowing him to pull her into his room and shut the door, remaining in his embrace for as long as she could. She'd always taken pride in the fact that she was independent and could take care of herself, but it felt so good to lean on him, she didn't want to give it up. But she needed to explain to him, and then everything between them would be out in the open. They could start down the road to whatever this would become with time and attention, hopefully a love story like her parents or in one of his books.

"I've got something to tell you." She pulled back, not letting go of him, but enough to where she could see his face. "I was asked by Babette and Saul Forasch to arrange a one-on-one fan experience with you."

"What? What does that have to do with you crying?" Micah's expression grew fierce, the ice in his eyes one of the rare glimpses of the Marine underneath his skin. "Did he… they hurt you?"

She shook her head. "No. Not really."

"I'm confused."

"I'm not explaining this very well." She took a breath and decided to reveal the worst of it. "I agreed to convince you to do the fan thing with her in exchange for their reference for the management program which would guarantee that I got the spot."

Micah pulled away from her, the loss of his warmth only surpassed by the glacial temperature in his eyes and the utter stillness of his body. He was mad and she didn't blame him, but nothing prepared her for the words he ground out between his gritted teeth.

"Was fucking me a part of the deal, or did you do that for free?"

...

It hurt like a motherfucker.

Micah couldn't believe that he'd been so wrong. Again.

"Micah, no," she stuttered out, her hand reaching out to touch him.

He dodged her; the last thing he wanted was her hands on him when he could still smell her on his skin. Retreating further into the room, he was surrounded by evidence of just what an idiot he'd been: rumpled sheets, empty wineglasses, and used condom wrappers on the floor.

Exhibit A to just how stupid he can be when he allowed his dick to lead him around.

"No, Kelsey. No," he said, not even bothering to keep his anger in check. "At what point did you decide it was okay to use me? Did it ever occur to you to ask me? Am I that big of an asshole that you didn't think to ask me? Fuck, I would have done anything for you."

She stared at him, her mouth moving soundlessly before actual words came out. "I knew you didn't want to do it. You said..."

"So you decided that orgasms would make me easier to manipulate?" He laughed, the bitter catching in his throat. "It's either food or sex, right?"

He carded his fingers through his hair, resisting the urge to throw one of the ugly but expensive knickknacks on the table across the room. That didn't help so he lowered his hand to his chest, rubbing the tightness just under his ribs, trying to ease the ache that he knew would blossom into bone-numbing pain later. This wasn't his first heartache rodeo.

Fool me once, shame on you. Fool me twice, shame on me.

He could not believe that he'd been so wrong about Kelsey.

"Micah, if you will listen for one fucking minute." Her tone was angry, frustrated. He had no idea why she was pissed—she wasn't the one who looked like a fool.

"I think that's been my problem. I've been listening to you for days now, and I bought it. Every. Single. Word." He moved toward her, looking her straight in the eye. To her credit, she didn't flinch. But he shouldn't have been surprised because she hadn't so much as blinked when she was working her little deal behind his back.

"I wasn't lying, not about us or what happened between us," she said. "The way I feel about you is real."

"Yeah, about as real as the shit I write in my books." He walked over to the door, placing his hand on the knob. He wanted her gone. Now. "You saw me as an easy mark, and you went for it. Kelsey, you told me from the jump that you were ambitious, and I didn't want to listen. I wanted this to be something that it was never going to be. Nicely played on your part."

"You're not listening to me. You have to let me explain," she said.

"I think I got it. I heard you and anything else you have to say is of no interest to me."

"Micah…"

She touched him. Her hand on his cheek, soft and tender and it took everything in him to resist leaning into her caress. He loved her. No matter how fake this had all been to her, it had been real for him. He couldn't remember feeling this way about Becky, and he'd wanted to spend his entire life with her. He'd been dreaming of a life straight out of one of his bestsellers forgetting that in the end it was only a work of fiction.

"Seriously, Kelsey, this whole thing is killing me here, and I want you to go."

He needed space, and he needed to get through this stupid ball tonight, and then he needed to get on a plane and go back to Bridger Gap. When he'd first gotten out of that bed in Germany after the bombing and placed his feet on the floor, it had felt like the world was shifting under him and any second he would be swallowed up and just…gone. The injury to his head fucked up his balance, and it took months of PT to finally accomplish the task of getting out a bed without landing flat on his face. This felt a lot like that, and he wanted her gone before he hit the ground—realistically or metaphorically.

"Micah…"

"Just. Go."

Kelsey dropped her hand, using the back of one of them to wipe the wet from her cheeks.

"I want you to know that I'd decided not to give them what they wanted, no matter how it impacted my reference."

"Is that supposed to make this okay?"

She shook her head. "I only wanted you to know. It might have started out differently but what happened between us was real and never about Babette."

He looked down at the floor, really wishing she'd go and leave him to pack, go to the stupid ball, and get on the first flight he could out of this town.

"Kelsey…" He left it at that. There was nothing he could say to change this shitty situation except to ignore the fact that she'd been lying to him for days, and he'd spent enough time living with his head up his ass.

She huffed out a sharp, painful sound that hovered between a laugh and a sob, and he lifted his head, immediately regretting his decision. The pain on her face was dark and deep, and the urge to pull her close was overwhelming. The moment he thought he might cave she moved toward the door, stopping to look back at him on the threshold.

"Look, I know I fucked this up, but don't forget that stuff we talked about last night. I know you want different things for your life and your career, but don't forget that you have options to do it all if you want to. The guy I know wouldn't waste the opportunity he's been given, the kind that most people would kill for." She leaned up and pressed a swift, hard kiss to his mouth, and Micah leaned into it, in spite of knowing better. When she pulled back, her eyes and face were fierce with the conviction of her words.

"You have a gift and your words impact people. You saw that yesterday with your fans. Don't waste it."

Chapter Seventeen

"You got fired?"

Kelsey flopped down on the lounge chair by the pool next to Sarina. Normally she would love the idea of kicking back by the pool on a day when she would usually be at work. Downtime was a luxury she hadn't taken advantage of in the last few years. Now she had all the time in the world.

"Yeah. I was cold busted fucking around with a guest. I knew the risk and I lost," she said, shoving the box full of her personal items to the side of the chair. "I had 'multiple orgasm hair' and was wearing my clothes from yesterday. Lying wasn't an option."

"Oh, Kelsey." Sarina leaned over and grabbed her in a big hug, tightening her hold when Kelsey started shaking. The goddamn tears were back, and she couldn't do a thing to stop them. Sarina was like a sister, her safe place, and she could fall apart with her and know that her secrets were safe. How many times had she sat in her bedroom, Sarina's apartment, or by this very pool and poured out all the shit about her mother that she could never tell her father? Too many times to count. Family wasn't only forged by blood—sometimes it grew from a liberal dose of laughter, tears, booze, and Ben & Jerry's. "Honey, what did Micah say?"

That made her cry a little bit harder. As she turned in her employee ID, emptied her locker, and was escorted off the property by a glowering Perry, all she saw was the look of complete and total disgust and hurt on Micah's face. She'd hurt him. She'd known she would—she just didn't know how much it would hurt her.

"It's over between us."

"What the hell?" Sarina asked, pulling back enough for Kelsey to see the shock on her face. "What do you mean it's over? You only got started."

"I told him what I did, how I had agreed to help Babette, and he couldn't forgive me."

"What an asshole."

She shook her head, unable to jump on board that train. "I knew what I was doing, knew the risk. He'd told me about being used by people, and I never had a doubt that he wouldn't take it well if he found out. If I had thought he'd be okay with it, I would have told him right off the bat."

"Sure. I don't disagree, but it's not like you murdered his puppy or something,"

Sarina's ivory cheeks were flushed with her anger, red splotches of color on her neck giving away just how pissed off she really was. Sarina wasn't hotheaded, no matter how many redhead jokes people made, but when she got really ticked off, you needed to duck and cover. Kelsey did not want Sarina going off on Micah—that would only make it worse.

"I violated his trust. I lied to him."

"But you didn't do it. You never handed over the goods."

"True. I decided that there was no way I could do it, but

that doesn't change the fact that I completely started our fling with a huge ulterior motive."

"When he heard you lost your job, he still kicked you to the curb? That's a dick move," Sarina cut her off when she tried to speak. "I'm sorry, it just is."

"I never told him I got fired."

"Why not?"

"Because in the end it didn't matter."

"Fuck that, Kelsey! He got you fired. It sure as hell matters," Sarina said.

"I got myself fired. Not Micah." She stood up and leaned over to pick up the box of items, anchoring it on her hip and squinting in the late-afternoon sunshine. "I was a big girl, and I took the risk."

"Oh, but Kels." Sarina stood and took the box, nodding her head toward Kelsey's apartment. In her high-heel sandals and swimsuit, her best friend looked like a pinup from the 1940s, the kind guys used to paint on the side of their airplane before they flew off into battle. She was strong, and Kelsey knew she would be leaning on her so much in the next few days. "You cared about him, I saw it on your face. It's got to be killing you."

Getting her keys out of her purse kept her face hidden, and she was glad for the excuse not to look at her friend. Losing her job was disastrous, potential financial ruination, but losing Micah cut to the quick, leaving her too raw and exposed for public viewing at this time.

"It is. I…" A deep breath, and she let it loose. "I fell in love with him, and I was hoping…"

She hesitated, knowing that if she said it out loud, it was somehow committing to the heartbreak. Fully admitting what she'd lost.

"Hoping?"

"I was hoping for the happily ever after in those books I love. I was hoping for the whole sappy, romantic, silly, movie-of-the-week shebang."

"Oh, honey…" Sarina's big green eyes filled with tears, and Kelsey turned away, opening her door in an attempt to stave off a crying jag. If her bestie started bawling, then she would, too, and that would just be too pathetic.

She grabbed the box from Sarina's hands and took a deep breath, turning her mind to how she wanted to spend today and tonight. Getting fired and dumped called for a night of drinking and debauchery. Luckily, she lived in the town that was tailor-made for nights you'd never remember.

"I'm in the mood to get drunk and vomit in some poor cabbie's ride. You in?"

Sarina's face fell, her frustration written in the slump of her shoulders. "I can't. I'm the only one working in the shop tonight. You want to come with me?"

Kelsey thought about it. A night at home, watching TV, and drinking alone or hanging out in a sex shop with her best friend and all the local perverts? It was no contest. She had a long time in the future to lie around and wait for her broken heart to heal.

"Sure. I'll let you sell me a new vibrator. I think I'm going to need it."

Chapter Eighteen

Saturday evening

one hour before the Romance Convention Ball

"I thought getting some regular tail was supposed to put you in a better mood," Allen said as he rummaged in the fridge of Micah's suite.

Micah faced his reflection in the mirror and cursed as the stupid bowtie refused to cooperate for the ninetieth time. He stripped it off and tossed it back on the bed, hating this stupid monkey suit, and the prospect of spending his evening dressed up at the closing ball to the convention.

He wanted to be gone, needed to be on the plane headed back to Bridger Gap and the life he lead before he fell for Kelsey Kyle and completely missed the fact that she was just like everyone else.

"I called your pretty little concierge up here to get your shitty attitude adjusted." Allen strolled across the living area, a beer in hand, and looking perfectly at ease in his tux.

He really hated him right now. "You did what?"

"I summoned your hot little genie in a bottle to come up here and chill you the fuck out." He laughed and thrust his crotch forward. "A little rub here. A little stroke there."

Murder. Swift and bloody. It would solve so many of his problems right now. "Allen, butt out. Kelsey and I are done. I don't need her, that's why I have you."

"I'm not sucking your dick, dude. The fifteen percent you pay me does not cover sexual favors."

"Allen."

"Yeah?"

"Shut the fuck up and listen to me." Allen smirked, completely unfazed as usual and motioned for Micah to continue at the same time he lifted the bottle to his lips. "Kelsey was using me. She fucked me in order to get a VIP guest one-on-one time with me in exchange for a guaranteed spot in the management program here at the hotel. It was never about me. It was never real, and I don't want her here."

Allen stared at him, the bottle poised in midair as he ran the data on everything Micah had just unloaded in the room. The shock he could deal with, but the last emotion that crossed his face was…pity.

"Dude, that sucks. I know how much you dug this girl."

"Yeah, well…"

The brisk knock on the door, followed by a louder, male voice stating "concierge" interrupted their conversation. Micah didn't want to get into a big heart-to-heart with Allen anyway; it would only put a glaring spotlight on what a fool he'd been.

Allen walked over to the door and opened it, allowing the tall, dark-haired man to enter. He was dressed in the male version of the concierge uniform that Kelsey had worn, but his nametag boasted he was part of management.

"Mr. Holmes, my name is Perry. I understand you requested assistance from Ms. Kyle but she no longer works here, so I came up to see if I could take care of your request."

Micah stared, not quite understanding what he thought he'd heard. "What do you mean that Kelsey no longer works here?"

Perry squinted at him, transferring his confused gaze to Allen and then back to Micah. "I meant what I said. She is no longer employed by this hotel."

"What? When did that happen? Did she quit?" He knew he wasn't giving the guy any time to respond, but this was a complete and total surprise. Kelsey loved her job. She had plans to move up the corporate ladder, and while she wasn't guaranteed a spot because of her failure to deliver him to Babette, that didn't mean she had to quit.

Perry now added "uncomfortable" to his expression, shifting slightly on his very shiny, polished black shoes. "If I can be blunt, Mr. Holmes, she was fired this morning when we discovered that she was…involved with you." He cleared his throat, not liking this conversation at all. "I presumed she told you when she came up here this morning."

Fired. Jesus.

"No, she didn't say a word about losing her job." Micah rolled it over his mind, their conversation from beginning to end. She'd shown up devastated by something, and he'd held her until she told him about using him. They'd argued, he'd been pissed, and ordered her out. Not a word about her job. "She didn't tell me."

"That's something I would tell right away," Allen said. "Talk about burying the lead."

"Yeah, no kidding." Micah looked at Perry. "You had to fire her? There was no probation, appeal?"

"No, sir."

"How did you find out? We were careful." He wracked his brain to figure out how they'd been seen. The only time could have been this morning, but they'd been sure she'd fly under the radar that early.

"She was seen leaving your suite this morning and it was reported by another guest."

"Another guest?" Allen asked, his voice full of disgust. "Who would care? It's not like Micah's got some girlfriend or something skulking around this place."

Allen was right; he had no one here who would care. No other guest who would go out of their way to report them to management. He stopped, looking at Perry when one name popped into his mind.

"It was Babette." Perry didn't even flinch but a very small nod confirmed his guess. "She was pissed because I turned down her offer of a three-way."

"A what?" Allen almost spit beer across the room. "Seriously, why does this stuff happen to you? You never take advantage of the gifts God dumps in your lap."

Micah wasn't going to debate the reality of God arranging a three-way for him with Allen. Ever.

Perry spoke up. "I don't know if you care, but Kelsey had the opportunity to keep her job." He cleared his throat again, regret taking over his expression. "I wish she could have taken the out, but I understand why she couldn't. The hotel…I lost a great employee today."

Micah was confused. "What could she have done? You said you had no choice."

"The guest who reported the two of you is very influential at the hotel, and they offered to not only speak to management about overlooking her violation of the policy but they would also give her the reference she needed for the management program."

"What did they want her to do?" Micah felt sick to his stomach. He knew.

"They wanted her to hand you over. One-on-one time and from what you said, it wasn't just for you to sit and read to them."

Allen snorted, and Micah threw him a dirty look. If he hadn't been in the mood for Allen's shit earlier, what he'd heard sealed the deal.

"She turned them down," he said, only a hair above a whisper.

Perry nodded. "Flat."

It took him two seconds to pull his head out of his ass. Perry turned and walked toward the door, opening it with a flourish as he tapped his Bluetooth device in his ear and spoke in a low voice.

Micah turned to find Allen grabbing his tux jacket off the back of a chair and slipping it on as he gave him a "are you kidding me?" look. "Of course I'm going with you to find her. If this girl can get you off that damn mountain once in a while, I'm her biggest fucking fan."

"Thanks, man," Micah said, pressing his hand to his shoulder. "I hope she'll give me another chance."

"Just do what the dudes in your books do, and you'll be fine."

"There's a cab waiting for you in front of the hotel," Perry said.

They hustled out of the hotel suite, beating feet down to the elevator. Micah's entire body was strung so tight he might break if someone touched him right now. He knew that feeling would not go away until he had Kelsey back in his arms, in his bed, in his life.

"Do you have any idea where she might be?" Allen asked as they stepped into the elevator.

"I think so. Either her apartment, her mother's room at Desert Rest, or her best friend's store."

"What kind of store is it?"

"A sex toy shop," he answered, pulling up Kelsey's phone number on the screen and making a call. He didn't expect for her to answer but it was worth a try. He pitched forward a little when Allan slapped him on the back.

"We're going to a sex toy shop? Really?"

Micah nodded, disappointed when Kelsey's voicemail clicked on. He ended the call. "Her best friend owns an adult book, film, and sex toy shop."

Allen hugged him, his voice muffled against Micah's shoulder. "You are the best friend I could ever have. You get to get the girl and I get porn."

Micah laughed in spite of himself, determination to make Allen's word come true replacing the doubt and worry in his gut. "Well, then let's go get my girl."

Chapter Nineteen

"What is this?" Kelsey asked, holding up the box she was pricing for Sarina.

Her friend's head popped up over the countertop where she was arranging the sales bags underneath. She glanced at the box and smiled, her look stating that it was exactly what she thought it was. "It's a pigtail butt plug."

Kelsey stared at the item for a moment. It was black, made of some kind of silicone, and had a curlicue pigtail on one end. It wasn't her thing, but it wasn't the weirdest thing she'd seen all night, so she slapped a sticker on it and grabbed the next one out of the shipping box.

"I have to say that the Alien Area 51 sex doll with the three breasts and suction cup fingers is my favorite."

Sarina choked out a laugh as she rose from behind the counter, letting her eyes linger on Kelsey. "You seriously do not have to work. You've had a shit day, your heart was stomped on. You can hang out and drink the wine we brought with us."

Kelsey looked around the store. It was busy, the Saturday night crowd either picking up things for a hot date or something to make going to be alone a little bit easier. A young, twenty-something blond-haired couple that looked like they belong in a Hollister ad held a leather spanking paddle and a ball gag. A big, hairy dude with two huge ear gauges and tattoos everywhere she could see was looking at butt plugs with his twink boyfriend and occasionally giving the loner guy dressed in jeans and a polo shirt the "would you like to join us" glance. She'd bet money that they'd all be trying out that toy later this evening.

The plan had been to go with Sarina, hang out, get plastered, and pass out in her office. Sarina bought the booze and promised a ride home. Perfect.

"Since I have to hit the pavement and find some work tomorrow, I can't afford to waste tomorrow hungover." She thought of her mortgage and her mom's care and a frisson of panic slithered over her skin. "I really can't afford it. I'll get throw-up-on-the-sidewalk drunk when I know I have income."

"Bury your heartbreak in work?"

"That's exactly what I'm doing," she said, trying to take a deep breath around the cold, burning lump of pain sitting on her chest. She had no idea that someone she knew for only a few days could become so vital, so essential to her happiness… but there it was. She'd have lots of time to regret her stupid mistake and losing the guy who had a shot at being "the one."

The bell over the door jingled and they both swiveled to see who was coming into the store. Sarina started in with her usual smile and "Welcome to Sizzle and Pop" when her grin completely dissolved, and she snuck a glance at Kelsey.

They weren't customers. It was Micah and his agent, Allen.

"Kelsey," Micah said, his expression lighting up at the sight of her. It made her glow inside too, a warmth that did a little to dull the pain. Hope jumped up into her throat and kept her from answering the question she heard in his voice.

"Unless you are here to grovel and kiss her ass you can get the fuck out of my store." Sarina charged at Micah, and everyone in the store swiveled to get a good look at the drama about to unfold in beautiful HD.

Micah broke eye contact with her, glancing at Sarina. The confusion on his face clearly showing that he was trying to process what she'd said. "Umm…yes…I'm here to grovel."

"Well, good…" Sarina lost some of her steam. "It better be good. I've read your books, and you get them down on their knees begging well enough."

"You're here to grovel?" Kelsey finally found her voice, standing and walking toward him, tossing the sheaf of price stickers in the general vicinity of the countertop. "How did you find me?"

"We've been all over this damn town," Allen said, speaking but running his hand with great interest over a lingerie set. "Your place where your buddy Aiden almost threw us in the pool, and then we went to see your mom." He tore his gaze away from the silk and lace outfit. "Sylvia says hi and that your mom had a great day."

"You went to see my mom?" Kelsey asked Micah.

"I checked in on her when I was looking for you. I thought you'd want to know how she was."

Anger bubbled up to mix with her happiness at seeing him again and for the second time that day, she had moisture welling in her eyes and blurring her vision. The highs and the lows of her emotional rollercoaster made her a little crazy. "Damn you, Micah Holmes," she yelled.

She grabbed a bunch of condoms from a bowl on the counter and threw them at him. She'd never been compelled to hurl something at someone's head before, but these past few days had been full of her doing things she'd never done before.

The rubbers hit his tux-covered chest and shoulder and slid to the ground, some of them getting snagged by the edge of his lapel pocket, a button or his waistband and hung out there like multicolored square-shaped confetti. He just stood there, poised to duck, as if he was waiting for her to latch onto the bowl and chuck that at him too.

"I told you he was Micah Holmes!" The blond-haired woman squealed and nudged her boyfriend in the ribs. She walked over to Micah and shoved the ball gag package into his hands. "Here's a pen. Can you sign this for me? I'm a huge fan."

Micah, his expression now completely confused, took the pen and scribbled his signature over the photo depicting a guy wearing the gag and full submissive leather gear while seated at the feet of an Amazonian-looking woman. He shoved it back into the fan's hands but never took his eyes off of Kelsey.

"Oh my God. Can I get a photo?" The woman squealed even louder than before, and that broke Micah out of his trance. He looked down at Blondie, an apologetic but exasperated smile on his lips.

"I'm in the middle of something. Can you wait?"

She shrugged, looking over at Kelsey before taking two or three steps away from Micah. He walked toward Kelsey, the condoms dropping to the ground and joining the one he stepped on as he made his way to her.

"Kelsey, I'm sorry."

"For what?" Yeah, she'd been wrong but he was an asshat too, and she needed to know exactly what they were both going to apologize for before they wiped the slate clean and started over.

"For not listening to you. For not letting you explain." He

took a deep breath and stopped right in front of her, close enough for her to see the couple spots on his chin he'd missed with his razor and the fluttery throb of his pulse underneath his skin. His words dragged her gaze back to his eyes. "Perry told me the whole story, and I'm so sorry. I understand why you agreed to do it…"

"It was awful."

He nodded once, acknowledging her mistake. "But you didn't do it, even when you had a chance to save your job and the management program." He stepped even closer, and now she could feel the warmth of his breath on her lips, smell the soap he used. She wanted to kiss him, desperately, but she wanted to hear what he had to say more. "You didn't do it."

"I couldn't." She licked her lips and tried to steady her heartbeat. Right now it was so fast she felt lightheaded—or that could have been Micah. "You were mine. I couldn't share you with her or ask you to do something I knew you wouldn't do."

"I was yours?" His voice was husky, ragged as his own chest rose and fell rapidly with his accelerated heartbeat. "Past tense?"

"You tell me." Kelsey knew it was cowardly to lob the ball back on his side of the court, but she needed to hear him say it. "You're the wizard of the words."

He laughed, his hands rising to cup her face as he leaned, a breath away from a kiss. She slipped her arms around his waist, her skin tingling all over from the contact.

"I probably suck at this way more than I should considering the books I write, but I'll give you the words you deserve to hear. I want to be yours, Kelsey Kyle. I *am* yours for as long as you want me, which I hope is a very long time." Micah closed the gap with a kiss so soft that she would have missed it if her entire being wasn't focused on him. It lasted less than a minute, but when they pulled apart, her heart was racing again, in a good way. "I was an idiot, and I'm sure I will be an idiot again, but I promise I will always grovel as soon as you tell me I'm wrong."

She laughed and wrapped her arms around his neck, taking his mouth in a kiss that burned hot enough to erase the stupidity of the last few hours. Kelsey knew she was missing out on prime ass kissing from a man who wrote the best in the business, but she didn't care. She always liked the happily ever after part anyway.

"I've fallen in love with you, Kelsey," Micah said.

"Oh, good. I thought I was the only one."

"Nope." He shook his head. "I'm crazy about you, and I want to make this work. I don't want to get on that plane tomorrow, I want time with you. Time for us. Can I have it?"

"It just so happens that I'm unemployed for the moment, and I have lots of time," she kissed away the frown that took over his smile for a moment. "And I would love spend it with you. I want that too…us…you."

He kissed her again, deep and wet, and she hopped up, climbing him like a tree until her legs wrapped around his waist. Micah groaned into her mouth, his large hands cupping her ass as he worked to keep his balance from her assault. The room around them burst into catcalls and whistles and clapping. It was ridiculous and she was happy and they broke apart laughing, her arms still wrapped tight around his neck. Micah's grin turned wicked and cunning.

"What?" she asked, wondering what he was planning.

"I was thinking about the fact that you're looking for a job."

"I don't want to think about that right now."

"But what if I told you that I have a proposition for you?"

"Better than the one you just made me?" she asked.

He cocked his head to the side and pretended to think about it. "I wouldn't say that, but you *would* get to work closely with an incredibly talented, sexy, and brilliant guy every day."

Kelsey narrowed her eyes, "Is there health care and an expense account?"

"*Everything* is on the table." She could tell by his eyes that he was offering more than a paycheck, and she wanted it all. She wanted…everything.

"Tell me more."

Epilogue

"What is that?" Kelsey pointed to the large object he'd just unpacked from the crates delivered to the condo earlier that day.

Shortly after the convention they'd both traveled to Bridger Gap to pack up his stuff and for Kelsey to meet his family. The family was as expected: wonderful, all loud and obnoxious and overwhelming and very excited to meet the woman who'd tempted him to actually feel all the things he wrote in his books. He was content to sit in the background with his father and watch the antics of the seven women in their lives.

Of course, she'd hit it off with the girls right away. His mother and sisters were like Kelsey, outgoing, driven, and determined to get everything organized and done with an efficiency that would impress the USMC. He'd stood by and followed orders when given, excited to pack up a life that had never felt like his own.

That life, the one where he *actually* lived and didn't sit on the sidelines, was now in Las Vegas in the *Melrose Place* condo that was currently in the middle of a major renovation. He'd purchased the unit next door, and the wall between the two was gone, the opening covered with heavy plastic. They needed more space if this was going to be their home and the office for his publishing company.

After several long talks with Kelsey and Allen, he'd decided to self-publish his military thrillers and write one romance novel a year for his publisher. So, now he was a CEO of a company with one sexy, smart, and talented employee. She was watching him, her expression reminding him that he'd never answered her question. "Are you asking as my girlfriend or as the Operations Manager for Bridger Gap Publishing?

She looked at him and then back at the model long-range missile standing in the middle of the floor. It stood almost to her full height and opened on a hinge so that you could see the components inside. In his opinion it was fucking badass, and more importantly, it was the weapon of mass destruction in his newest novel. Research…it was research.

Kelsey considered his question, crossing her arms on her chest and biting her bottom lip in concentration. It reminded him of last night on the kitchen floor when he fucked into her slowly, drawing out the pleasure as they christened another room in the condo. She'd insisted on it when he'd agreed to move in with her, explaining that it would give them good luck for the future.

He'd told her that they didn't need luck, they had a winning hand no matter the odds, but he would never pass up on sex with the woman he loved. But now she looked like she wanted him to drag his precious memorabilia to the curb instead of strip off her panties.

"Well?"

"My answer depends on whether you want to put it in the living room or your office," she said.

"Okay." He laughed, liking how her mind worked. "I'm answering my girlfriend."

"Then I say hell no you are not leaving a mock weapon in the living room." She held up her hand and scooted away when he stood up and started tracking her around the room. "And that answer won't change no matter how many orgasms you promise me."

"Do I get a different answer if I ask my most valuable employee?"

"Nope. No weapons in the living room or the bedroom or the kitchen. Just no." She tried to dodge his grasp, but he was faster, using his longer leg span to catch her near the front door.

Micah pressed her back to the foyer wall, capturing her lips in a kiss he hoped would lead to something more fun than unpacking all these boxes. Kelsey seemed to be very open to the unspoken suggestion, her mouth opening to his pressure on a sigh, her fingers sinking into his hair to pull him closer. He was hard already, the constant state of his body anytime his gorgeous girlfriend was in the same room with him. The total package of beauty, brains, and bravado, she excited his body, made his heart pump with life, and gave him the courage to take a leap of faith in his life and his career.

It was fast. They were fast. Many people thought it was crazy, but they knew. Both he and Kelsey knew that what they'd been holding out for was living and breathing between them, and all they had to do is keep it alive. It was the easiest and the hardest thing he'd ever done, and it was worth it. He woke up every morning knowing that it was worth everything.

When he'd decided to self-publish his military thriller books, he knew he needed help. A right-hand person who could help him stay organized and be his rock when he had to tackle the fan stuff that still made him want to cut and run. He couldn't imagine doing it without her anymore…Kelsey had spoiled him for anyone else. She'd agreed on one condition: that he'd write one romance with his publisher every year for his loyal fan base.

He'd agreed to write the book, but it would be for her, his most important fan. Best. Hiring. Decision. Ever. And as soon as the time was right, he was going to give her the small velvet box he had hidden in his sock drawer and change their status one more time. The last time.

They broke apart and Kelsey murmured against his lips, "Is this part of the enhanced benefits program you mentioned when you recruited me to work for you?"

"Are you kidding? This *is* the enhanced benefit," he laughed and dove back in for another kiss just as a loud knock on the doorframe interrupted them.

They didn't jump apart, merely turned to see which one of their friends was visiting. Aiden, Liliah, and Sarina were in and out of here all the time. Micah had quickly realized that it wasn't a condo complex; it was a commune with a pool.

"At least you guys aren't naked in the pool again," Sarina grumbled from the doorway, holding out a gift bag from her store, the Sizzle and Pop logo emblazoned on the side. "This is a congratulations-on-getting-laid-on-a-regular-basis gift from Aiden, Lilah, and me. Since we all love the story of how you guys met, we figured this could be a fun reminder of that moment. It's waterproof, so you could use it in the shower or…" She flicked a humor-tinged glance over shoulder toward the pool and slid her cool, green gaze back to them. "Well, you'll figure it out, I'm sure."

Micah released Kelsey just enough for her to reach for the bag and press a kiss to Sarina's cheek in thanks.

He kept his arms loosely wrapped around her waist, smiling at the redhead who played it cool all the time. She never broke a sweat or got flustered, and he wondered whether she was really that together or if she pushed it all down. Still waters and all that…usually ran deep with pain or loss in his experience.

"Thank you, Sarina. I'm sure we'll enjoy it," he said, jerking his head toward the living room. "You want to come in?"

"Nope. I have to get to the shop and I'm sure you'll want to break in the new bed you had delivered this morning." She smiled and waggled her eyebrows as she backed out of the doorway to leave. "Don't forget to do *everything* I would do!"

They watched her leave, and Micah tried to peek in the bag, but Kelsey pulled it out of his reach. "What is it?"

She opened the bag and looked at the gift, her eyes flaring wide as a huge grin spread across her face. He leaned forward to take his own turn but she snapped it shut, shaking her head slowly as a naughty grin spread across her lips.

"You're not going to let me see what's in the bag?" he asked, allowing her to duck around him and start to back down the hallway toward their bedroom.

"Nope," she said, reaching up to pull the scrunchie from her hair and tossing it to the floor. She shook her hair out in the way she knew made him itch to hold it tight in his fist as he fucked her.

Kelsey was deliberately teasing him.

He liked it. No. He loved it.

"I love you, Kelsey Kyle," he said, never tiring of the fact that he *could*.

"I love you, too." She didn't stop her achingly slow, sexy backward progress down the hall. "But that won't get you a peek into this bag."

He shut the door, twisting the lock and taking two steps forward when she cranked up the pout and got all of his attention with her sexy, seductive purr.

"In fact, you won't get to see what's in here until you're naked and on the bed," she said, her voice teasing but firm. She smiled wickedly at him and his cock got harder at the naughty promise in her gaze. "Just leave your clothes by the door, you won't be needing them tonight."

"You know," he drawled, slipping his T-shirt up and over his head and then tossing it to the ground at his feet. His jeans joined them and he sped up his pursuit of Kelsey, spurring her to turn and dash down the remainder of the hallway. "I remember you telling me the same thing one time before."

"And look how well that turned out for us."

And as Micah followed her into their room, he couldn't have agreed more.

About the Author

Robin Covington loves to explore the theme of fooling around and falling in love in her bestselling books. Her stories burn up the sheets...one page at a time. When she's not writing she's collecting tasty man candy, indulging in a little comic book geek love, and stalking Chris Evans. Don't send chocolate... send eye candy!

Robin's bestselling books have won the Golden Leaf Award and finaled in the Romantic Times Reviewer's Choice, the Book Seller's Best and the National Reader's Choice Awards.

She lives in Maryland with her handsome husband, her two brilliant children (they get it from her, of course!), and her beloved furbabies.

SEDUCING SEVEN
a *What Happens in Vegas* novella by MK Meredith

CALLING HER BLUFF
a *What Happens in Vegas* novella by Kaia Danielle

Also by Robin Covington

THE PRINCE'S RUNAWAY LOVER

A NIGHT OF SOUTHERN COMFORT

HIS SOUTHERN TEMPTATION

SWEET SOUTHERN BETRAYAL

PLAYING WITH THE DRUMMER

PLAYING THE PART

SECRET SANTA BABY

SEX AND THE SINGLE VAMP

Printed in Great Britain
by Amazon